THE
FAMILY FRYING PAN

Bryce Courtenay is the bestselling author of *The Power of One*, *Tandia*, *April Fool's Day*, *The Potato Factory*, *Tommo & Hawk*, *Jessica*, *Solomon's Song*, *A Recipe for Dreaming*, *The Family Frying Pan*, *The Night Country* and *Smoky Joe's Cafe*. He was born in South Africa, is an Australian and has lived in Sydney for the major part of his life.

Further information about the
author may be found at
www.brycecourtenay.com

BRYCE COURTENAY

THE
FAMILY
FRYING PAN

ILLUSTRATED BY
ANN WILLIAMS

PENGUIN BOOKS

Penguin Books Australia Ltd
487 Maroondah Highway, PO Box 257
Ringwood, Victoria 3134, Australia
Penguin Books Ltd
Harmondsworth, Middlesex, England
Penguin Putnam Inc.
375 Hudson Street, New York, New York 10014, USA
Penguin Books Canada Limited
10 Alcorn Avenue, Toronto, Ontario, Canada, M4V 3B2
Penguin Books (NZ) Ltd
Cnr Rosedale and Airborne Roads, Albany, Auckland, New Zealand
Penguin Books (South Africa) (Pty) Ltd
24 Sturdee Avenue, Rosebank, Johannesburg 2196, South Africa
Penguin Books India (P) Ltd
11, Community Centre, Panchsheel Park, New Delhi 110 017, India

First published by William Heinemann Australia,
a part of Reed Books Australia 1997
This revised edition published by Penguin Books Australia Ltd 2001

3 5 7 9 10 8 6 4 2

Typeset in 11/15 pt Times New Roman by Post Pre-press Group, Brisbane, Queensland
Printed and bound in Australia by McPherson's Printing Group, Maryborough, Victoria

National Library of Australia
Cataloguing-in-Publication data:

Courtenay, Bryce, 1933– .
The family frying pan.

Completely rev. ed.
ISBN 0 14 029341 8.

I. Williams, Ann, 1942– . II. Title.

A823.3

WRITERS' BLOC

THE READER IS ALWAYS RIGHT

www.penguin.com.au

To my two sons Brett and Adam
who would not be who they are if their
great-great-grandmother had not
walked across Russia carrying a
large cast-iron frying pan.

AUTHOR'S NOTE

When this book first appeared it was designed as a series of interconnected short stories which, when taken all together, became a novel. This seemed to me to be quite a nice idea at the time. It was a different-looking book, richly illustrated in colour and black and white by Ann Williams and with a recipe suggestion at the end of each story.

In retrospect I suppose it was a bit of a hotch-potch, neither fish nor fowl, so that booksellers didn't quite know what to do with it. Was it a book of short stories? Did the colour illustrations suggest it was a young person's book? Perhaps even a cookbook? Or was it a novel in a form they'd never seen? As it turned out, they could never quite decide, with the result that my publishers felt that the book had not received the attention it deserved.

Finally, the editors at Penguin Books persuaded me to see if by rewriting it, eliminating the colour pictures and the recipes and by rewriting the front and the back sections and some other parts of the narrative I could put it into a more conventional format for a novel.

The Family Frying Pan is not so changed that if you have a copy of the original you will need to purchase this one. But if you've never read it, I must reluctantly conclude that I think this is the better of the two versions. I shall miss the glorious colour pictures and the recipes but we have retained the delightful black and white illustrations, which I think give this book a lot of character.

Like a great many of my stories *The Family Frying Pan* is based on the truth. Mrs Moses did exist, she did walk across Russia carrying a large cast-iron frying pan on her back and she was the early morning scourge of Bondi Beach. Moreover, she is the original inspiration for the book and these are her stories, given always that in the folk-story genre fact and fiction are identical twins. I hope you will enjoy her adventures.

ACKNOWLEDGEMENTS

As always in the making of a book there are others to thank. Benita Courtenay, not only for gifting me her Jewish family and with it the incomparable Mrs Moses, but also for always being there. Kay Ronai, my editor for this version of the book, and Clare Forster, my publisher. I neglected in the original book to thank Margaret Gee for her considerable help and do so now. Finally there is Ann Williams who did the illustrations and whose black and white etchings continue to enhance this edition.

INTRODUCTION

When I married into my wife's family I inherited her grandmother, Mrs Moses. That's what she was called by everyone in the family, not mama, or mum or nana or buba or even grandmother, simply Mrs Moses. My in-laws referred to her in this way and even addressed her as Mrs Moses. Her first name was Sarah, though she'd been Mrs Moses for so long I doubt whether her own daughter remembered her name. There was nothing cold or formal about this appellation, nor was it intended as a sign of respect. Mrs Moses simply couldn't be called by any other name and still remain herself. From the age of sixteen and unmarried, she had been known as Mrs Moses and it had been ever thus. How this all came about is a part of her story.

Mrs Moses was a famous identity around Bondi Beach. Every sunrise of the year, except for those which occurred on a Friday, would find her ploughing across the sand in her droopy black old-lady bathing suit heading for the surf. Pelting rain, gale-force winds fierce enough to bowl her over, as they often did, waves crashing down, throwing spume and angry spray at the shoreline, it made no difference. At dawn Mrs Moses was ready to bathe.

When, on occasion, the beach was too dangerous for swimming, the king tides smashing against the sea wall, she'd use the handle of her walking stick to knock on the door of the Bondi Lifesavers Club until someone forced it open against the wind and the rain.

'You call this weather!' she'd sniff, shaking a tiny bony finger at whoever appeared. 'From weather you know nothing, young man, in Russia is weather, here is only a bit of raining and winds, now you must open the beach at once so I can bathe!'

Mrs Moses also gathered people like a farm girl might gather eggs, stepping out every morning with an empty basket and returning with it full of new-made friends.

'You got a name?' she'd say, walking directly up to an early morning bather or stroller. 'So tell me, already? Maybe I remember so next time you're not such a stranger. Me, I'm Mrs Moses.' She'd stretch out her tiny claw, 'Pleased to meetcha, Mr Big Nose. Name please?' she'd demand again.

It was her special trick. Well into her eighties (how well she wouldn't say), she never forgot a name, first name or surname. Forever afterwards she'd pass someone to whom she'd introduced herself and say, 'Such a nice morning, Mr Big Nose, Peter Pollock, or Miss Nice Legs, Julie McIntosh, or Mrs Big Boobies, Tania Walker, or Mr Noddy Ears, Eddie Perrini, or Mrs Fat Bum, Sarah Jacobs.' She would greet each with such a disarming smile that it became impossible to take exception.

On her return from her early morning dip in the surf, she'd stop at the skateboard ramp and demand that the action cease immediately, 'Stop, already!' she'd shout, rapping her walking stick against the side of the wooden ramp. Whereupon she would distribute a five-cent piece to every kid on the ramp, 'Go buy a nice ice-cream,' she'd say, 'enjoy, compliments Mrs Moses.'

The skateboarders happily accepted the tiny

silver coins and thanked her politely, no one daring to tell her that a single vanilla cone now cost a dollar. In fact, if she ran short, as she often did at times during the school holidays, there'd be a real look of disappointment on the faces of the non-recipients of her largesse. The five-cent coin from Mrs Moses became a status symbol for the skateboarders, to be collected and kept in the pocket of their board shorts to jingle during a tricky turn or backward somersault. Larry Hinds, the Bondi boy who became world skateboard champion, jingled his way to the title with a pocketful of her ice-cream coins. When he returned to Australia he presented Mrs Moses with his world championship T-shirt, which she wore ever after as her nightgown.

Mrs Moses claimed to be five feet and two inches tall though towards the end of her life she was probably under five feet. Nevertheless she stood straight as a pencil and, except for a bit of a pot on her old-lady stomach, she was in pretty good shape.

'From sixteen years and now eighty years and something – don't-ask-it's-none-of-your-business – and still only thirty-five kilos,' she'd say, patting her tummy lovingly. 'Eat once every day only a little.' She'd cup her hand, indicating the amount.

'The greedy die young, it's God's revenge for not sharing the food with others.'

When her granddaughter brought me home to introduce me to her family, my future mother- and father-in-law were concerned that the boy their only daughter announced she was going to marry was not Jewish nor seemed to have any real qualifications and even fewer prospects. 'A writer already. How can a writer make money in Australia?' my mum-in-law-to-be protested. Like all Jewish mothers, she was hoping at the very least for a doctor or a lawyer.

However, Mrs Moses had no such concerns, she accepted me immediately, mostly because I *was* a storyteller and in her mind there existed no higher status. I was soon to learn that in the storytelling department I was a rank amateur compared to her.

Friday evenings it was compulsory to attend family dinner to celebrate the onset of Shabbat, the beginning of the Jewish Sabbath. Despite the prayers, candles and truly awful wine, nothing could have kept me away. Mrs Moses made the best Friday fried fish in the whole of the universe.

I recall on one occasion sitting with the old lady on the back verandah under the bougainvillea enjoying a glass of her homemade ginger beer. Two rosellas were yapping away in the mass of deep scarlet blossom above our heads, the southerly had just blown in across the beach, bringing with it a cooling down after a long hot day. Mrs Moses had cooked the fish earlier in the day but its delicious smell still pervaded the back porch. Even then I fancied myself as a bit of a cook and so I asked her, 'Mrs Moses, how come your fried fish is the best I've ever tasted? What's the big secret? Is it that you always use snapper? Or is it the batter?'

She'd fry it in a light beer batter, snapper caught that morning and bought straight from the Doyles' fishing boat. The fish was the reason she never got to the beach of a Friday. Instead she'd be up at dawn in time to catch the first bus into Bondi Junction to connect with the one to Watsons Bay, arriving to greet the Doyles' fishing boat coming into the pier soon after sunrise.

Always first in the queue she'd inspect the catch with a wary eye and finally choose a big snapper, keeping a beady eye on the scale as it was weighed and then immediately protesting at the price, demanding that she pay the same per pound as she'd paid their father thirty years before. 'Shame on you! Your father should turn in his grave, he should know what you're charging me!'

With a suitable amount of objection and a collective show of consternation, all of this accompanied by much sighing and shaking of heads, the Doyle brothers finally gave in, the same fish-bargaining ritual of every Friday morning of their lives played out. They had long learnt that the first snapper they hauled in every Friday was for Mrs Moses and that it was going to cost them money. Irish, and therefore superstitious, they'd come to think of her fish as a sort of tithe to the sea and, like the skateboarders, they saw Mrs Moses as an essential part of their good luck.

The old lady would carry her catch home on a repeat of the double bus trip, the great fish with its body loosely wrapped in newspaper, the exposed head and tail spilling over the edges of her wicker basket. The bus conductor would step down onto the pavement at the Watsons Bay terminus, take up the basket and place it on a vacant seat next to the window, then he'd open the window. 'Fresh fish don't smell from nothing!' Mrs Moses would snap, 'For your breath we should open a window, this fish I can kiss!'

'I should charge you double, Mrs Moses, that fish takes up more room than you do.'

'All day walking up and down, "Fares please, fares please", this is a job for a nice boy? Double? You want to charge double!' She held up one hand with fingers splayed and the thumb showing from the other. 'The fare has gone up six times since I come first here sixty-five years ago. What we got here, Mr Fares Please, Tommy Johnson, is daylight robbery, no less. Maybe I write to the Prime Minister!'

She'd be home before nine when she'd clean and fillet the large fish, saving the head and the tail for fish soup (also unequalled), and then, well before noon, she'd have completed frying the great white flaky fillets in a golden batter so that they were presented cold for the evening meal, and served with red-rimmed Spanish onion rings and pickled cucumber doused in a sharp brown vinegar sauce.

'The snapper? You think it's the snapper? Snapper, batter! A fish is a fish, Batter also. Flour and egg is flour and egg. A little beer added maybe, salt. I tell you somethink.' She leaned her head slightly towards me and crooked her finger, indicating I should come closer. 'It's The Family Frying Pan!'

She said it reverently and like that was its proper name, The Family Frying Pan, in capital letters. Then she whispered, 'It has a Russian soul.' She turned and looked at me, 'One day after I die you will write the story, please. Maybe a whole book.'

'The story?' I asked, not knowing quite what she meant.

'The story of The Family Frying Pan.' She drew back, her eyes suddenly misty, 'My story, I have told no one, only now you.'

THE POGROM

In Tsarist Russia the Jews were not, as a general rule, among the wealthy classes but mostly existed in small rural villages which were known as *shtetls*. Most of them worked the land and were in every way a peasant class, though the Russian peasants, themselves devout Russian Orthodox Christians, were deeply anti-Semitic and, even after hundreds of years of living side by side, resented their presence. It became a common practice for Cossacks, the Tsar's elite mounted troops, to raid a Jewish village for no other reason but an afternoon's sport. They would come charging into the village on horseback and set about murdering all the inhabitants and burning the houses and the small synagogue before moving on. Whatever local authority existed turned a blind eye, it was always open season for killing Jews in Russia and while the Russian peasants were forbidden to do so, the Cossacks could do as they wished. A raid on a *shtetl* was therefore thought of as an afternoon's entertainment and as a cleansing of vermin from the Motherland.

One of the highlights of this 'game' was for two mounted Cossacks each to take up a mewling infant, holding it by its ankles. Then both horsemen would retire to opposite ends of the village and, on a given signal, gallop towards each other, swinging the baby around in the air, the idea being to use the infant as a club to knock the opposing baby from the grasp of the opposing horseman. If the heads should connect, splitting the soft cranium of the infants so that their brains splattered across the flanks of the horses and the uniforms of the Cossack riders, there was much applause from their fellows, good horsemanship and the mastery in the saddle being prized above all other virtues.

The village in which Mrs Moses lived as a sixteen-year-old servant girl in the house of the rabbi was raided by the Cossacks, and all the village's inhabitants, some two hundred souls, were killed, Mrs Moses being the single exception. Sent into a cornfield by the rabbi's wife to pick fresh corn for the evening meal, she'd seen the Cossacks coming towards the *shtetl* and had hidden until they'd left just after sundown.

She knew that she must flee immediately, the Russian peasants would soon enough descend on the village and take what they could find, stripping the garments from the dead and taking what bits and pieces that had not been destroyed then setting fire to the village. Mrs Moses knew that if they found her they would kill her instantly.

Standing among the ruins of the village, wisps of smoke and small fires still burning, Mrs Moses decided that she would attempt to walk out of Russia to find a place in the world where soldiers didn't kill children and where 'Jew' wasn't a dirty word pronounced with venomous spittle through clenched teeth.

It was deep into autumn and Mrs Moses had no idea how long it would take to walk out of Russia, but with winter almost upon the land she did not possess a warm coat. Furthermore, her cast-off shoes were worn through, the uppers cracked.

For such a journey she quickly realised she would need both coat and boots in good condition. Mrs Moses looked about and soon found the body of Mrs Abrahams, the village know-all. Mrs Abrahams owned a good pair of boots, which had been fashioned out of the best leather available by the village

14

bootmaker for her daughter's wedding just two weeks previously.

Standing over the dead woman, Mrs Moses addressed her politely. 'Mrs Abrahams, this is Sarah Moses, you don't know me but I know you, I was a kitchen servant to Rabbi Rabin, and also an orphan whom he took in when my parents were killed in a previous pogrom. As you can imagine, there is no future for me here now and I know God will help me to walk to freedom in your nice new boots much admired at your daughter's wedding. I thank you for your generosity, may you dance in heaven wearing a pair of golden slippers.'

Then Sarah Moses looked around for a good coat and soon enough came across Mrs Solomon. Brushing the flies from the dead woman's mouth, she explained, 'Mrs Solomon, the good Lord will keep me warm but on this occasion he needs a little help from you. A helping hand no less, one final act of charity from someone who was never very famous for her charitable works. When you arrive in paradise may you wear a cloak of peacock feathers that fall from your shoulder all the way to the ground.'

With Mrs Abraham's new boots on her feet and

Mrs Solomon's excellent coat on her back, she knelt in the ashes of the destroyed village and said a prayer. 'Lord, with the help of Abraham the Patriarch to guide my feet and the wisdom to wear a warm coat that comes from Solomon, maybe I got a good chance to make it out of Russia. I ask Your blessing and Your guidance.'

Then she rose and turned to the dead Mrs Solomon. In the good boots and fine warm coat Mrs Moses felt very grown up and confident as she looked down at the dead woman who was now wearing only a light cotton shift. The flimsy garment had ridden up to show her knees and thighs so that Sarah Moses adjusted it, speaking to her as she pulled the hem down to Mrs Solomon's ankles. 'I am sorry, my dear, but there are not ten good male Jews present to form a minion to say the *Kaddish* for you and also Mrs Abrahams. When I get out of Russia, I promise I will pay a rabbi to say the prayer for the dead for the whole village and with a special mention of your generosity and also Mrs A.'

After making this promise, Mrs Moses walked over to the rabbi's house where she fossicked among the smouldering ashes until she came upon a very large cast-iron frying pan. It was a pan much used in the household for it was large enough to embrace a meal for five or six people, maybe even more. Picking up a rag, she wrapped it around the still hot handle of the frying pan and, using both hands, plucked it from the warm ashes. Then, looking heavenward, she pronounced, 'I swear to God that the generations to come who eat from this pan will taste no more the bitter fruit of life.'

While the boots and the coat made perfect sense, the heavy cast-iron frying pan seemed a curious thing for her to choose to take with her on her journey. After all, she had a whole village of dead people's things to choose from, stuff she might barter on the way, yet she chose a pan she could barely lift and nothing else.

The frying pan had a hole at the end of the handle through which she threaded a piece of rope, tying it in a loop that she strung around her neck so that the pan would rest against her back. Sarah Moses then put on Mrs Solomon's coat, which gave her an altogether curious appearance. The weight of the pan pulled her straight as a ramrod yet she appeared to have a curious hump to her back when she walked. She had no clear destination in her mind, but thought only to walk away from the cold and out of Russia forever.

There is a time in the history of almost every nation when those who are in power are so removed from the common people that they have no sense of their suffering and, finally, their anger. They are oblivious to the foment around them and cannot see the signs of their own demise, which in retrospect will have been obvious.

These were the years before the revolution when the frozen roads out of Russia were filled with the starving, the dispossessed and the hungry. All were trying for a new life, not only Jews, but people from every faith and social background, who, because of their foolishness, politics, dreams or misbegotten ambitions, had been marginalised. They were the gypsies of despair on a road to nowhere they could name other than that it should be some place beyond Russia where they could once again nourish the seeds of hope. They came from every part of the mother country, preferring to die on the rutted road to freedom than to starve in the dark cellars, the rat holes of the great cities. It was among this peripatetic throng that Sarah Moses now found herself.

They would walk in small groups, spending the day fossicking for scraps. Mrs Moses would search for twigs until, by nightfall, when they stopped to huddle together so that they might keep warm, she had gathered a bundle sufficient for a fire. 'Come around, friends,' she would shout at all and sundry, 'I have a good fire and a fine frying pan, God will supply the rest.'

It stands to reason that on some occasions she would have gone hungry but that's not how Mrs Moses tells it. Her story has it that someone would reach into the interior of a shabby coat and produce an onion, someone else would find a couple of potatoes in the pockets of a pair of threadbare trousers, a few cabbage leaves would appear from inside the blouse of one of the women, then a jar of fat or a small lump of meat from somewhere else. Soon enough there'd be a meal bubbling in the pan that would be divided equally among them, Sarah Moses careful to keep the smallest portion for herself. The Family Frying Pan, with a little help from the Lord, never failed her. With a few warm scraps in their stomachs, the mood would lift and a violin would appear and they'd sing the melancholy songs about Mother Russia and starvation when the crops failed or when the Cossacks came and they'd cry a bit and tell stories with sad endings.

And so the days progressed through the first harsh winter and into early spring. They had stopped for the night and the usual fire was going with The Family Frying Pan set upon it, the scraps gathered during the day just coming to the boil. Sarah Moses had removed Mrs Solomon's coat and had used it to wrap around a baby who had been born to one of the women in the group two days previously. Though the sun had set, it was not yet dark and people were moving about in the vicinity of the fire, ready to settle down for the night, when around a turn in the road about two hundred metres away appeared a troop of Cossacks.

It took only a moment for those around the fire to react and only a moment longer for the soldiers to turn their horses in the direction of the fire and to come charging in, striking at the motley group with their swords and clubs. People were running towards the protection of a small wood, screaming as they were cut down. Sarah Moses seemed to be the only one among them to somewhat keep her head, though what she did next would seem foolish enough to have cost her her life. She snatched The

Family Frying Pan from the fire and emptied its contents on the ground and slung it by its rope into its accustomed place about her neck. Such was her panic that she didn't feel the pain as the rim of the pan burned through her dress and seared the flesh of her back. Next she removed the baby and, placing it beside the fire, she put on the coat. Finally, gathering the tiny infant in her arms, she began to run.

By now she was well behind the rest of the fleeing people, some of whom had reached the safety of the dark woods. Others lay dead where they had been stabbed or clubbed down, their blood flowing into the rutted road and filling the hoof marks, their brains splattered in the muddy soil.

The captain of the troop, wearing a high plumed helmet and gold epaulettes on his long grey military coat, galloped furiously up to the wildly fleeing Sarah and stabbed his sword into her back as he dashed past. Its blade snapped instantly and the impact of the suddenly halted blow sent the captain flying out of his saddle and over the head of his horse to land on his head, snapping his neck and killing him instantly under the furious hooves of the oncoming horses.

Sarah Moses was also sent flying by the blow from the sword but somehow she managed to cling to the baby as they rolled together in the mud. As she struggled to her feet, almost instantly a second horseman swung at her with his mighty club, sending her sprawling, though still she held onto the tiny infant. The blow from the club should have killed her instantly for it was aimed at the centre of her back, to snap her spinal cord.

In all the yelling, screaming and the whooping of the Cossack troopers, the *clang* as the club struck the metal of the frying pan went unheard as did the anguished cry of the trooper as his wrist snapped and his club fell to the ground. Again Sarah Moses rose and continued to run and again a third horseman struck at her with his sword, to repeat the performance of the captain, breaking his neck.

Rising once again, she managed to reach the safety of the woods.

From where they hid within the dark woods, some of the travellers who had managed to escape from the Cossacks witnessed the attacks on Sarah Moses. Not only had she made it to safety but two great swords had snapped like matchsticks as they attempted to pierce her body, and a club had bounced off her harmlessly. Moreover Sarah had clung to the baby throughout the terrible ordeal and had brought it with her unharmed. The infant, covered in mud, now suckled happily enough at her mother's breast.

They immediately declared it a great miracle and after a minimum of discussion pronounced Sarah Moses a living saint. They concluded that she had been sent by God and pointed to the fact that her name was Moses no less, the same as the great patriarch who had led the children of Israel out of the land of Egypt. It took only a tiny leap of imagination to see Sarah as his reincarnation, sent to lead them safely out of Russia. There was only one small catch, Moses was a married man and Sarah was a sixteen-year-old girl and it would be difficult in the Russian language to find a patronym which extended to her the correct amount of respect. So, after a little more discussion, they simply dubbed her Mrs Moses.

When in 1986 Mrs Moses died and my mother-in-law deemed it unseemly for her to travel to the funeral parlour in Larry Hinds' T-shirt, my mother-in-law dressed Mrs Moses in a fresh linen nightgown and, while doing so, saw for the first

time a curious scar on her back that formed a perfect circle across the breadth of her tiny body.

And now, as Mrs Moses told it to me in her own
words, here is the story of how she led her people
out of the wilderness . . .

THE SEASONS

The seasons in Russia are not like Australia where, in most places, the differences between summer and winter don't merit the possession of an overcoat.

However, the preoccupation Mrs Moses had with the weather is as much a part of her story as anything else. Spring was hope, summer was life, good and bad, autumn was at first beguiling but then became a warning of misery to come, and winter meant death.

So that the story of The Family Frying Pan can truly be told I must tell you about the seasons in which it took place. Using a tape recorder and with only a minimum of grammatical correction, mostly because spoken words are not placed in quite the same way as when we write, I have put them down as the old lady spoke.

I found her words to be beautiful. It was as if she had practised them all her life, polishing them, sounding them, rounding and smoothing each on her tongue until they became more than language and carried within them the essence of Russia at that time before the revolution.

Spring

It has been a lovely spring day, still cold, for the ground has not fully thawed, though the sun is bright enough for hope to leap like skipping children into our hearts. The streams in the woods, last remembered as muddy pools in the late summer, now rush with the blue melt of snow and, even though the ground clanks like iron when you stamp your feet, stiff green shoots of daffodil and lily-of-the-valley push through the frozen mud. The sap rises in the forest so that the branches, the small tender branches, show tight green buds at every extremity. High in the sky a lark sings and the breeze carries the first scent of honeysuckle and almond blossom.

SUMMER

It is the sunsets, always the sunsets, that make me feel that the day on the road has been worthwhile. That the dust and the flies and the muddy puddles after sudden rain, the turgid rivers and the heat are bearable as we walk our road to freedom. Russia is such a big country, such an endless place where walking all day seems to bring you to the same spot. And everywhere the struggle to stay alive, so much space filled with so much pain.

It is easier to find food, and the gold of the ripened corn stretches so far across the horizon that its reflection burnishes the sky. Summer evenings are an enchantment, that part of the day when Mother Russia rests her burden for a few short minutes to dip her brush into a palette of ripened wheat and then to paint the sky with the burning colours of hot, urgent life.

AUTUMN

The autumn days are beautiful, mellow and tranquil at first. There is a ripeness about everything, a proper conclusion to all things. The sky is a serene blue and there is a feeling of restfulness in us all. But then things start to brood, at first a little sulky, or in polite language, a trifle melancholy as the heat begins to fade and the days to shorten. Finally impatient and spent of energy by the long, hot summer, the mood darkens and a sense of malevolence, of unease, thickens the air.

The wheat and the corn are harvested, the fields shorn, scythed clean, emasculated, husked and exhausted. The sky glows the colour of old pewter and the leaves, the tears of the dying forest, begin to drop silently to the ground. The wind now comes from the north like a shrill whistle through clenched teeth. A fine rain falls, misted spray that seeps into our clothes and squelches through the broken leather of our boots. The sun weakens and grows pale as though seen through algid water and the air is stale and still. Darkness comes suddenly, with a cluck of the tongue or the snap of malevolent finger and thumb.

WINTER

God has gone absent from Russia, left us to fend for ourselves, defeated by the endless snow, the malice of the howling wind, the remorseless ice drifts, the bone-white horizon bleak beneath a firmament where the stars have turned off in a vacant sky that offers not the slightest hope.

We plod on when we can, stiff legs wrapped in rags, but for the most part there is no winter journey in this ghost landscape. We've stored what little food we have, a bag of flour bargained for with bits and pieces we still possess, it must last against these evil, endless months. We are rats gnawing on anything we can find. The old people die and our tears are frozen irritations against our cheeks. Death is such a constant visitor that we can only sigh, it brings a mouth less to fill and the threads taken from old backs can now be used to cover younger, stronger bones.

Winter in Russia is the white wolf of suffering and each day we dread its howl and fear that it will run us down, that it will rip and tear and devour, so that we will not make it to the end of this stark and terrible bleakness.

SOMEWHERE
IN RUSSIA

We have made the evening fire and all of us have gathered what twigs we could find on the day's journey. Now it has burned down to the embers. My famous Cossack-defying frying pan, with a dob of lard, sits spluttering and spitting on the soft glow. The meal, as usual, will be turnips, potatoes and onions. And, if we are lucky, maybe a little red cabbage, all of which will be scavenged by my fellow travellers and given willingly at the day's end to be shared among us. Occasionally, a scrawny old winter-worn rooster is bargained from a peasant for a kopek or two, or a nest of field mice or a clutch of quail eggs is discovered. These are happily dumped into the pan. But mostly it is the same, and with it what's left of the rough, coarse ember bread we bake at dawn for the day's travelling.

'What shall we have tonight?' I ask my fellow travellers. 'What delicious concoction, splendid banquet or magical meal? What delectable and memorable supper, special treat or delight to assault the nostrils, what delight to send our taste-buds into a frenzy and to seduce our palates?'

And always someone will raise a hand. Some-times a learned professor, or a musician, a chef's wife, a seamstress, a blacksmith, a scholar, two lovers or even a circus acrobat. It doesn't much mat-ter. In the business of food there is no pecking order and all come equally to the table of the imagination.

'Ah!' someone will say. 'How well I remember dining with the Tsar, His Imperial Majesty himself. And, of course, the Tsarina and the five girls and Prince Alexei, the heir to the throne. Let me hasten to add, this was not a State occasion, only a simple meal with a few close friends in a smaller ballroom in the grand palace in St Petersburg, no more than two thousand present. Such a cosy little feast.'

'The recipe story!' we will all urge at once. 'Tell us what we will be tasting tonight!'

And so the recipe storyteller will begin and we begin to feel the delicious salivation of anticipation. The contents of the pan, now bubbling on the fire, will soon be ready. We will share the food, the turnips and potato and onion and cabbage, perhaps only a few spoonfuls each. But, ah, what spoonfuls! For we feast on the words of the storyteller and, if words can make a stomach contented, by journey's end we will all be plump as partridges.

SUCH A CLEVER
LITTLE MUSHROOM

Anya puts up her hand tonight. She is a thin woman with a sad face, perhaps in her late twenties or much younger even. Russia and a poor marriage make short work of a beautiful bride. Yet there is still something left. Her eyes are blue as cornflowers and there is a fullness to her lips and, surprisingly, none of her teeth are missing and they are white and perfect, so that her smile is serene and angelic. At night she will sing to the children with a voice like a thrush and she loves to read aloud. It is as if her books are good friends which she must share with us, for Anya has love to give to all. Her baby is the infant, wrapped in Mrs Abraham's coat, whom

I scooped up when the soldiers of the Tsar attacked. She is in love with Mr Mendelsohn, the violinist, and their love, even out of wedlock, is pure and clean and beautiful. Often she will gather wild herbs and mushrooms in the fields and woods and add them to our humble evening fare to make a feast out of a turnip, or turn a potato into a prince of vegetables.

'I shall tell you of my wedding feast so that we may choose a dish to eat tonight, a soup to serve to a prince,' Anya says as we sit watching The Family Frying Pan bubbling on the fire.

She sighs and begins her story:

I was chosen to be the bride of the landowner's only son, a peasant girl to compensate for a blood-line that had lost its vigour. My husband-to-be was a poor specimen, with eyes too close and hairy brows that joined across the bridge of his nose. He was rich and needed a male heir, and I was strong and, I suppose, pretty enough. Besides, it was an honour my father, who was a poor man, could not afford to turn down. So, for a good horse and a small cornfield, I was sold to the landowner's son.

As for myself, I was given no choice in the

matter. Love was not a word used easily in our village and the honour and good fortune bestowed on me was thought by all to be most profound. The old women would cackle in my ear, 'He is ugly, Anya, but think nothing of it. In the dark, between the sheets, who is to tell pretty from ugly? Give him a male heir and one to spare and you can grow fat and live in comfort for the rest of your life.'

The wedding day came and the fat priest joined us together in a chorus of hymns and vows and prayers to bless our union with male offspring. Then we sat together alone at the wedding feast, my husband and I, while the villagers danced and feasted in our honour and we had nothing to say to each other.

The silence built like an abyss between us as the dancers whirled about us and the village men got drunk on good vodka. The fiddlers played love songs and the old women ogled the ugly groom and smacked their toothless gums at the thought of the splendid wedding cake to come. Some begged me to sing but the laughter and the song had left me.

'Why did you marry me?' I asked my husband at last, my heart thumping like a Tartar's drum at the boldness of my question.

'You have broad hips and big tits,' he snorted.

'There will be milk in your breasts for the male children you will give me. I have seen you carry a burden worthy of a mule, and I am told you can cook to delight a man's stomach. I desire no more from a woman, save silence and obedience.'

'But I can read to you,' I cried. 'I alone among the village girls can read and I have also a little Latin and the new art of Botany!'

'I have no time to listen, nor you to pleasure yourself with books of which we shall have none in my house.'

'Then I shall sing to enchant you?'

'It is enough that the birds sing when they steal my corn. What will you steal from me when you sing?'

'Shall I play the harp then?' I asked him. 'The harp to rest your soul when you are weary.'

'Vodka will do that task well enough, the harp is for idle fingers and your hands will not be idle for any waking moment of the day. You will rise at the cock's crow and you will be last to bed.'

'What then, my husband? How then shall I please you?'

'You will cook and clean and fetch and carry and remain silent and breed my many male children and feed them on your paps until they are three years old. If you do all of these things well, you will not be beaten more often than is good for you.'

'What shall I cook to please you most?' I asked, trembling.

'There is a chicken soup my mother used to make as thick as a plate of stew and seasoned with fresh herbs from the fields and wild mushrooms from the forest. It is the aromatic herbs that make the difference. Do you know these herbs, woman? Can you make this soup?'

'Every village girl knows them. The soup, too; I shall make it for you, but not as well, I dare say, as your sainted mother.'

'You will make this chicken soup for me every night and serve it silently and with humility. If it is not as good as the soup my mother makes, you will be beaten, for my mother says it is this soup of herbs and wild mushrooms and plump chicken meat that gave my father the vitality and vigour to conceive a son as splendid as me!'

And so I made the soup a thousand times, each time more delicious than the last. The years rolled by and the landowner died and I had to call my husband 'lord'.

Each night he would sniff at the soup. 'Not the right smell!' he would yell. 'A scrawny chicken no less!' Then, often after wolfing down each bowl, he would beat me. 'Not as good as my mother made!' he would shout as he knocked me down. 'It is the herbs! You have the herbs in the wrong proportion.' He would point to my flat belly. 'You eat my bread and, see, you remain barren, you are cheating me of sons, of male offspring, you are nothing but a miserable village whore!'

Then one night he sniffed imperiously at the bowl and I waited for his admonishment, but he said nothing. When he had slurped his soup like a pig at a trough and wiped his mouth with the back of his hand, he looked at me, his beetle brows dark and twitching, his small eyes black and hard as agate. 'Perfect! The aroma perfect, the chicken perfect, the herbs in all the right proportions! Tonight, woman, you will bear me my first son!'

That night as he mounted me he was taken quite suddenly with a great gnawing pain in his belly and was soon overcome with a terrible vomiting sickness. 'You have poisoned me with my mother's chicken soup and what's more you have failed to give me a son, I have no heirs, my good name is lost forever,' he screamed between the sharp spasms of pain.

'No, my lord, the soup is good,' I protested. 'It is your mother's soup, made just the way you like it, perhaps a pinch more salt, nothing else.'

'Call the doctor, woman!' he groaned.

The doctor came in his top hat and fancy horse and buggy and shook his head. 'Call the priest!' he shouted.

The fat priest came and prepared the sacrament and heard my lord's final confession and then gave him the last rites. I was standing behind the priest so that I might hear my husband's words of regret, the sins committed and the absolution so generously given.

'Forgive me, Father, for I have sinned, I have sometimes beaten my mule too hard and I have not always given a full measure of corn to those who till my fields!'

'God is merciful, my son,' the priest intoned, 'the pain in your stomach is sufficient penance, besides a mule has no soul and is a stubborn creature at the best of times and is known to try the patience of a saint.' The priest licked his lips. 'As for the peasants, it is their lot in life to be cheated by the landowner.' He made the sign of the cross. 'You could this very night enter the gates of paradise, my son.' The priest paused, coughed and then continued, 'This I can guarantee if you leave a little thought for God's kingdom on earth. Our coffers are empty and we need a gold cross set with precious stones, rubies and diamonds and pearls from the Caspian Sea. A cross so that all who come to pray for redemption will know we are a parish of the utmost importance in the eyes of heaven itself.'

'I am poisoned, I shall die!' my lord screamed again, pointing a trembling finger at me. 'She has poisoned me, she must be made to rot in hell, you must name her a witch!' His fingers clawed at his fat, hairy stomach and the blood ran from the corners of his mouth. But the man of God seemed not to hear, he was writing out a contract, his quill scratching out a last will and testament. In his mind the priest could see a gold cross, the afternoon sun streaming through the stained-glass windows of the church to reach the golden crucifix and set the gems upon it to blaze with the passion of Christ Jesus our Lord.

It was the midnight hour and the silver moon peeping through the window was as large as a melon when at last the priest held the paper out for my lord to sign. Groaning, my stricken husband, now absolved of his earthly sins and about to enter the gates of paradise, reached for the pen. But before he could hold it in his trembling fingers, he suddenly recovered. The pain which a moment before had torn him apart was quite gone, plucked like a mouse from a tussock of grass by the sharp talons of a hawk. What was about to enter the gates of heaven was back on the road of life again.

'A miracle!' the priest exclaimed, clapping his fat hands together. 'Sign here on the dotted line! God, in his infinite mercy, has spared your life! You must repay Him at once!'

'Ah! Not so fast!' my lord said, shaking his finger at the priest. 'If God had needed my money for a golden cross, He would have allowed me to recover *after* I had signed your paper!' He grinned happily at this shrewd observation, his small eyes mean and cunning, and I could see he was very pleased with himself. Then, with a wave of his hand, he dismissed the holy father. 'Go now, priest, I shall send you six bags of corn for the poor.' He pointed to the door. 'Go, go, or will you stay to witness how I shall beat my perfidious wife for her bad cooking?'

And so the priest departed in the moonlight, cursing and shaking his fist at the house, and my lord beat me until I was black and blue.

And then on the dawn of the fourth day, after he had so miraculously recovered and when all around had seen his good spirits and witnessed his health completely returned, my lord rose from his bed as the cock crowed in the yard and loudly called for borscht, sweet tea and cinnamon rolls. But before a morsel touched his lips, he fell to the floor at my feet and all this was witnessed by three workers who had brought in the milk for churning. My lord tried to rise, but his body was strangely paralysed. The three village men carried him into his bed, their eyes as big as vodka glasses.

The men responded to my tearful and hysterical pleas to call the doctor and departed in haste, leaving me alone in the bedchamber.

'I blame you, witch!' my lord croaked, but he could say no more, his tongue was lolling, swollen and useless from the corner of his mouth.

'Ah!' I said, quite calm, so that I spoke in a most respectful whisper. 'Lord, do not blame me, blame the songs that have not been sung, and the music that has not been played, and the stories in wise books that have not been read beside the firelight. Blame the herbs from the fields, the secret herbs that can keep a girl barren if she chooses. (Did your sainted mother not tell you of these?) Finally, blame the wild mushrooms from the forest that make such a delicious soup, all the safe and the dangerous members of the fungi family. Let me tell you about them, the good ones and the bad.

'The tiny red mushroom with white dots you see in all the fairytale books, *Amanita muscaria*. (Did I not once tell you I knew a little of Latin and Botany?) It is what the shamans of the Koryk tribe in Siberia call the *wapag*, the name they have given to the tiny tribe of fairies and goblins, elves and pixies that inhabit the land of mushrooms and toadstools. The Koryk use the *wapag* to cast magical spells which turn the mind into seeing things that are not meant to be observed, devils and demons and other phantasmagorical hallucinations.

'Then there is the Liberty Cap, *Psilocybe semilanceata*. It too produces a state where dreams mix with reality and is popular among the more educated priests and is much used by them to frighten and then to trick gullible nobility into making donations to the Church.

'There is also the Poison Chalice, *Entoloma sinuatum*, a very toxic look-alike and often mistaken for an edible mushroom. But not by me, my lord, for I have fed you none of these, only the good and the beautiful have gone into your chicken soup.

'Ink Caps, to bring a flavour of nuts. The giant puffball, sweet and delicate. *Amanita caesarea*, Caesar's Favourite, the most delicious of all, usually found under beech trees, a subtle and sublime mushroom that turns a competent soup into a triumph of the soup-maker's art. All of these and more I hunted and found and prepared lovingly for you, all the good and none of the bad, and my best efforts were met with a scowl, a pig's grunt and often enough a severe beating.

'Now let me tell you about my little treasure, *Amanita phalloides*, the Death Cap, a fungus usually found under an oak tree. It has a sweet smell, though a little too sweet if you ask me, not unlike lamb's urine. And what a lovely deception it carries, for it has a pleasant nutty flavour, or so it is said, for I have not myself tasted it. But, of course, I forget, you two are by now four days acquainted. Did you not compliment me on my chicken soup just four nights ago? The famous chicken soup that was to bring you a son and heir. It was the very first compliment you have paid me and so I am not likely to forget it, or *Amanita phalloides* which allowed me to please my husband just once in my entire married life. It was a soup, you said, just like your mother used to make and you called for a second helping.

'And now perhaps there is just sufficient time for me to explain to you how this pretty little fungus works. First it makes you sick so that for six hours you vomit all the good food you have stuffed into your fat gut until there is only green bile and pain. Pain so great that you beg God to let you die. And then, six hours later, a miracle! A cure sufficient to give you the strength to beat your wife mercilessly. And then, three days pass, the mule is beaten again, the corn measured short, and normal life resumes. And, along with it any suspicion of foul play, so that all swear to your robust good health and give praise to God for a miracle to be credited to their own church, performed by their own holy Father Markovitch.

'Then comes death, silent as a cat's footfall. This time there is no mistake and the prince of darkness comes too quickly for the doctor in his horse and fancy buggy or the priest in his dirty cassock with white spittle at the corners of his mouth, his wine and host bread in a box under his arm along with paper, ink and pen. This time, my dear husband, there is only sufficient time for these few words of comfort from your loving wife.'

I bent over him and, with the ball of my thumb, closed his staring, lifeless eyes. Then I went to find two kopeks to place upon the lids.

'Such a clever little mushroom,' I sighed.

THE FEAST OF
PEARLS

It is Mr Mendelsohn who has put up his hand to tell a story tonight. We are all somewhat surprised, for he is a man of few words and what little conversation he has beyond politeness is reserved for Anya, the pretty mother of his infant son.

Mr Mendelsohn's lack of conversation is not missed because his violin speaks for him with an eloquence that no human tongue could possibly emulate. Each night at the fireside, after we have 'feasted', we are transported away from Russia, from tyranny, hunger and despair to a land conjured from his fingers and his bow. A land where children play without glancing over their shoulders and men are not slaves to a harsh landowner but find regular work for decent wages and their women till the fields and keep enough of what they grow to feed their families.

We all watch a little warily as Mr Mendelsohn puts away his violin. Such a careful man, he lays it neatly and with a sense of love and respect into its scuffed and scruffy case, as though he is laying to rest a much loved friend. For a moment we see his long fingers caress the brilliant lacquered instrument and then seat it within the faded velvet lining, before the lid comes down like a coffin and snaps shut. Such an unprepossessing case to house so eloquent an instrument. The violin, which has come to be a living part of our journey, a part of the glow of the firelight and our sweet rest from the weary day, will be silent tonight and we are all a little wary that the story he tells will not make up for this.

Mr Mendelsohn coughs nervously into his fist. 'I shall tell you of the Feast of Pearls,' he says. He coughs again and looks up at the stars as though he is remembering.

'I once lived for a short time in a fishing village on the shores of the Black Sea where palm trees grow and the flowers of the tropics bloom, and yellow butterflies as big as your hand flutter against a cloudless sky.'

'Here in Russia? Palm trees, tropical flowers, blue skies, butterflies? Surely you are misinformed,' cries Professor Slotinowitz, who, by the way, is not only a refugee from the Academy of Science in Moscow but also from the imagination. He thinks only in facts and what he calls logical deduction. Sometimes with his school-teacher ways, a real pain in the behind that one.

'Perhaps I have not got the words?' Mr Mendelsohn says, uncertain.

'No, no!' we all yell and I say quickly, 'The words you've got are already perfect! Such lovely words, tropical and butterfly words, and words warmed by the sun, continue if you please, Mr Mendelsohn!' We all glare at the professor of know-everything-without-any-imagination-to-save-his-soul.

Mr Mendelsohn still looks uncertain. 'I know I am not good with words,' he stammers and his eyes go to the violin case and his voice grows uncertain. 'I can play this place for you. I will let my violin tell you of the evening breeze like rushing waves through the palm trees and the splash of colour made by the butterflies in the shining midday air. With my bow I can paint the brash, exaggerated colours of the tropical blooms and the slap and shush of warm waves that spill and crackle on foamy silver beaches in the moonlight.' He reaches eagerly for his violin case.

But Anya places her hand upon his elbow. 'Your words are like jewels in the sun, my lover,' she says quietly, 'you must continue.'

Anya seems to give Mr Mendelsohn fresh courage and he starts to speak again. 'In this village on the shores of the Black Sea the fisherfolk push their boats out to sea when the stars are still bright in the firmament and dawn lies quietly asleep beyond the horizon. They fish all through the heat of the long day, and in the evening as the sun is setting they return with their small boats filled to the gunnels and glinting with the minted silver of fish.'

'What kind of fish?' Professor Slotinowitz demands to know.

'Shhh!' we all chorus, a rudeness for which we must be forgiven because the professor is such a know-all sort of a person that sometimes in the name of good manners we are forced to be rude to him. Only Olga Zorbatov is his equal in the clumsy-remarks department and you'll hear some more about her later.

Mr Mendelsohn blushes. 'Alas, I must beg your pardon, Professor. I know nothing of the kinds of fish and cannot tell a sardine from a cod.'

'Fish will do nicely, Mr Mendelsohn,' I say kindly and then turn to the professor and address him quite sharply. 'Thank you very much, Professor Sloti-know-all-o-witz, the fish mentioned in Mr Mendelsohn's story have gills and tails and silver scales and that is quite enough to know about them!' I turn back and nod to Mr Mendelsohn to continue:

Well, one day, not long after first sunlight, when the boats had been out no more than two hours, they were seen returning to shore.

The women mending nets, baking bread and tending to their children, came running down to the water's edge to see whatever could have happened to bring their menfolk home so soon.

They watched as all the small boats converged on one boat and the men jumped out into the shallow waves. They were lifting something from one of the boats and crowded around the burden as though anxious to share in the pride and glory of their catch. They waded up onto the wet sand and then they parted to show four men carrying a mermaid.

The mermaid's silver tail was flapping in great agitation, changing colour with every twitch so that the women were forced to shade their eyes from the furious flashing brilliance. The expression on her face showed clearly that she was not in the least pleased and the sounds she made were not unlike the mewing of a newborn kitten, not at all elegant, and contrasting rather badly with her astonishing beauty.

Now everyone knows what a mermaid looks like, but few people have actually been close enough to one to see what a truly beautiful creature she is. This mermaid had perfectly scalloped scales that changed to every colour in the spectrum at her slightest move, and which graduated from the size of a large silver coin at her waist to less than a small child's pinkie nail where her tail fanned out.

The skin above her waist was, in appearance, completely human, unblemished and as soft to the touch as the ermine lining of the Tsar's coronation crown. Around her neck the mermaid wore a perfect string of blue pearls. Her wet hair hung in swirls to her shoulders, dark as midnight, framing a milk-white oval face into which were set eyes of a luminous green that shone with the fire of cut emeralds. Where it might be supposed her nose would be petite with perhaps the slightest upturn to complement such a sublime face, it was nothing of the sort. In fact, it was somewhat imperious, a trifle too large, a commanding nose, a nose for a princess, no, not a princess, more like a queen. Her lips were generous and shaped like a cupid's bow and, while she seemed in no mood to laugh, the glimpse of her teeth allowed by her angry mewing suggested they were as perfect as South Sea pearls.

Mr Mendelsohn clears his throat. 'There remains only the delicate matter of . . .' He begins to blush furiously, clearing his throat again and then coughing into his fist. He looks over at Anya for help but when he sees her feeding his baby son, the infant's tiny greedy mouth sucking and smacking on her wet nipple, he takes courage.

'Her, er . . . breasts!' His voice is hardly above a whisper. 'They were perfectly shaped cones of sheer delight, rounded like the crescent moon and each crowned with a small rosebud.'

'Tush! Mammaries and nipples!' the professor snorts. 'There isn't the least thing romantic about such female appendages! Cows have them in any number, sows too, cats and dogs and stoats and weasels! Udders give me the shudders and tits give me the . . .' He pauses. 'Well, anyway, it rhymes!' He points to the little violinist. 'You play a commendable violin, Mendelsohn, but you tell a most improbable tale.'

The professor rises slowly, his hand on his rheumatic hip, and, leaning on his walking stick, he starts to walk from the fire, then pauses and turns back. 'If it were my story and I were you, Mendelsohn, I'd slice your mermaid neatly in half, make a damned good fish pie out of the bottom half and use the top half as the prow of a sailing ship, which I'd sail straight over the horizon all the way to America!'

The professor glares at me for a moment as though challenging me to reprove him again. 'No offence, Mrs Moses, but we need schemers not dreamers to get us out of this mess! The murder story Anya told last night was exactly what we needed to whet the appetite! A nice bit of chicken-soup revenge to lighten the burden of our journey out of Russia! To use a fishy metaphor, I would rather go hungry tonight than listen a moment longer to this load of codswallop! Good night to you all!' Then he stomps off, snorting like an old rhinoceros into the night.

I must say it took a lot of encouragement and not a little cajoling to get Mr Mendelsohn back to his story of the Feast of Pearls. And to tell the truth, we were to regret our efforts, for once he got started it was much of the same again. The artist in Mr Mendelsohn forbade him to miss a single detail. The colours and shapes of the clothes on the washing line of a house they passed carrying the mermaid back to the village, a fish hawk eyeing them balefully from the top of a tree, a brief dog fight, two black and red beetles mating on a tropical leaf. And, so much more, until the turnips, potatoes and cabbage in The Family Frying Pan were overcooked and still we hadn't come to the Feast of Pearls. It was going to be a long, long night and I could see everyone was beginning to envy the professor's decision to go to bed, even though they would miss the evening meal in the process.

I proposed that we stop to eat and then allow Mr Mendelsohn to continue. Who was to know that a man who spoke so seldom had all those words in a great reservoir inside his head? But they were there all right, a lifetime of unspoken observations which now bubbled over the dam wall in his brain and caused a verbal flood that overwhelmed us all. By the time he had completed his story all but Anya and myself had long since fallen asleep beside the fire.

For the sake of a neat ending I will try to tell you the rest of the story as quickly as possible. The mermaid proved to be not such a good idea after all. For a start the village possessed only the *mikvah* bath tub, that is the bath used by the women for ritual cleansing when their time of the month came, and she took possession of it. Moreover she had the most enormous appetite and consumed a large portion of the fish brought in every night. Her mewing never seemed to stop except when she sang.

Now, if you believe in the legend that mermaids lure lonely sailors to their doom on the rocks with their beautiful singing, forget already that theory. According to Mr Mendelsohn, the opposite is true, the sound is so raucous that the sailors, fleeing with their hands over their ears, are unable to steer the boat, which then crashes willy-nilly onto the nearest available rocks.

Well, to cut a long story short, the men in the village soon saw their families going hungry and, of course, they decided to throw the mermaid back into the sea. But that's where the trouble started. Happily housed in the village *mikvah*, fed like a queen every day, the mermaid had no intention of leaving. So when the men came to take her back to the sea she let out a single high-pitched sound that popped the eardrums of the six fishermen allocated the task. This caused a great consternation in the village until someone pointed out that since these six good men were permanently deaf they could transport the mermaid back to the ocean without fear. But when they entered the small room where the bathtub stood, the mermaid flashed her emerald eyes, and the rays coming from them were so fierce that the six fishermen were instantly blinded.

In desperation the villagers decided to starve the mermaid, but soon after she missed her first meal she began to sing. The sound was so awful that small children started to vomit, dogs went crazy, chasing their own tails and yowling, and men and women buried their heads in the soft sand or dived underwater, so that they might experience a few moments of relief. Soon they capitulated and gave the mermaid an entire day's catch.

This was the state of affairs when, one evening, Mr Mendelsohn found himself tuning his violin under the window where the mermaid was housed.

Now you will agree that the tuning of a violin can be a most unpleasant experience for the human ear, but not so, it turned out, to the ear of a mermaid. After a few moments of catgut scraping, the mermaid's face appeared at the window, and it was obvious she greatly liked what she heard.

Mr Mendelsohn, seeing her pleasure, played a few perfect notes on the violin, whereupon the mermaid's emerald eyes grew dark and her expression showed her displeasure.

So Mr Mendelsohn followed with a few strokes of the bow that sounded like a rooftop caterwauling and, at once, the mermaid clapped her hands in glee. Using every discordant note he could summon, the little violinist set to playing and the mermaid began to splash and cavort in the *mikvah* tub until she couldn't contain her pleasure a moment longer. She leapt from the bathtub out of the window to pirouette on the very end of her wonderful fishy tail, which flashed and gyrated as she danced in a frenzy of delight to the terrible screeching and squawking and scraping of the violin.

Instantly Mr Mendelsohn made for the shoreline with the mermaid dancing behind him. When he reached the water's edge he continued until only his shoulders and the violin were free of the waves, and the mermaid, as though in a trance, followed him.

Once in the water she began to swim in a circle around him, sometimes rising out of the water and leaping joyously in an arch over his head. It was plain to see that she had fallen hopelessly in love. Suddenly she stopped and, with her tail dancing on the crest of a wave, she took the string of pearls from about her neck and placed them over Mr Mendelsohn's head and kissed him.

It was a kiss so sweet that Mr Mendelsohn forgot that he was meant to play terrible rasping sounds and, quite transported by the mermaid's kiss, started to play the Brahms Violin Concerto. The mermaid was so horrified by this sublime music that she covered her pretty ears and dived deep down into the waves and was never seen again.

I looked at Mr Mendelsohn and shook my head. It was late and I would need to be up at dawn to bake bread in the pan for the next day's journey. 'So tell me, Mr Mendelsohn, I do not wish to be nosy but you have straw stuffed in your boots, half a dozen patches in your britches and your elbows stick out of your overcoat, what happened to the mermaid's pearls?'

I admit it was a bit forward and no doubt a little cheeky, some might say even rude, but it was well past my bedtime and I was too weary to mind my manners.

Anya opened her blouse and there, draped about her neck, was a magnificent double string of pearls which glowed in the moonlight. 'There are ninety-nine only,' Mr Mendelsohn explained. 'One pearl I took and sold so that the fishing village could buy new fishing nets, and a boat with a donkey engine and have a great feast, the Feast of Pearls, to celebrate the departure of the mermaid.'

'So, you are a rich man already, Mr Mendelsohn? Tell me, please, why do you travel with us? You could take a train and travel first class and eat three meals a day and smoke a Cuban cigar, and be out of Russia in three weeks, never mind nobody!'

Mr Mendelsohn sighed. 'I do not care for money, Mrs Moses, only music and love and a desire for freedom. I have all three of these treasures in our little travelling group. When we get out of Russia, Anya and the baby and I will go to America, the land of the free, and there I will sell the pearls and buy the Boston Symphony Orchestra, where I will be the First Violin until the day I die.'

THE PRINCESS TATIANA
AND THE
INDIAN MYNA BIRD

Professor Slotinowitz is up early and comes upon me just as I am laying the second batch of small wheat loaves into the frying pan to bake. Five loaves already lie on their backs to cool on a small muslin cloth. We will eat them during the day's journey and, with our evening meal, it is just sufficient to keep us from starvation. As for the rest, we hope always to come across a patch of wild berries, or an apple orchard with fruit on the ground from an overnight windfall.

It is surprising what may be found in a summer and autumn landscape. Locusts have a nutty taste, but can only be eaten when the bitter-tasting head and the papery wings are removed. A clutch of birds' eggs eaten raw is a gourmet discovery and fat grubs that live under the bark of fallen oaks and elms and lime trees are also delicious. The acorns we gather we grind for coffee and they can be eaten raw when there is nothing else. Roasted chestnuts are a forest delicacy, and all make life possible in the summer and autumn, but spring with all its bright promise yields very little to the hungry gatherer. Winter brings us nothing but the bitter cold.

'Good morning, Professor,' I call, not stopping to shake his hand, as my own is floury from kneading the bread dough.

'Humph!' he replies, clearing his throat. Then he adds, sotto voce, 'I apologise, Mrs Moses.'

'Whatever for?' I ask, knowing, of course, but determined to make him suffer a little longer.

'Last night, that stupid story, I could not contain myself.'

'Not so stupid as it turns out,' I say mysteriously, 'but very interesting, Professor, you should have stayed for the end.'

'Impossible! Dreamers have ruined my life. Impossible, ridiculous, impractical, stupid, irresponsible, selfish and thoughtless dreamers!' he pauses and sniffs. 'The bread smells good!'

I cut a warm loaf in the centre and hand one half
to the professor who had missed his meal when
he'd stormed out during Mr Mendelsohn's mermaid story. 'It's not extra, Professor, that is your
ration for the day,' I say firmly, then I point to the
kettle bubbling on the fire. 'There is coffee made
from ground acorns. You have your own cup, yes?'

'Oh yes, thank you, yes, yes, very good of you.'
He seems overly grateful as he produces an enamel
mug from the pocket of his worn overcoat. I pour
him a cup of the dark, bitter-tasting acorn coffee,
which is often enough all there is to get us started
on a cold morning.

He takes his bread and coffee and seats himself
on a fallen log. Then he reaches inside his coat and
produces a knife and fork. A red bandanna also
appears and he fluffs it in the air before arranging it
neatly on his lap. Placing the small half-loaf on the
cloth he commences to cut it into tiny squares and
eat it as though it were a meal of sausage and potatoes. His manners are correct and come from the
city, and he sits with a straight back as he chews
each tiny square thoughtfully, as if it were the
aforementioned sausages, or even the most delicate
cut of beef or some other exquisite morsel.

When the meal is completed I watch from the corner of my eye as he upturns the crumbs from the cloth on his lap into his cupped hand. Then he moves a small distance from the fire where he stands with his hand held out high above his head. It is still very early and the air is misty blue and not yet sharpened by sunlight. The professor's breath is smoky as he stands perfectly still, a tall man with a pointed beard and glasses, every inch the mathematical genius, very much the great scholar.

I continue to work, watching the bread and the coffee kettle and feeding twigs to the fire. I have half a mind to reprove him, even the smallest crumbs are treasures when you are hungry, and here the professor is holding the crumbs in the air and offering them to the wind as though he is carrying out some religious benediction.

He is also making a soft, breathy whistling sound which could be a prayer, though I would never have thought him to be the praying type. So it is with some amazement when I see the first small bird alight on his hand and then, in a few moments, half a dozen more flutter down out of a clear blue sky and come to rest on his now overcrowded palm. They begin immediately to chirp and quarrel amongst themselves as they compete for his delicious offering.

You could have knocked me down with a goose feather, but I told myself it was none of my business. You soon learn when you are travelling in a group to observe well but to remark little on the doings and affairs of the others.

It takes the birds no time at all to polish off the crumbs and so I wait for the professor's next trick. These are not very substantial birds but every little bit makes a difference and the professor is, to say the least, a pretty poor scavenger and makes almost no contribution.

The birds are now hopping on the old man's shoulders and his head and all he has to do is pick them off one at a time, squeeze their heads between his thumb and forefinger and drop each in turn into his pocket. Today such a cruel thought would not occur to me, but I have a full belly and a warm bed to go to. Starvation is not a condition which calls for sentimentality.

But the professor does no such thing and as each of the tiny creatures hops onto his hand he kisses the downy feathers and lifts them into the air to send them on their way. Soon all the birds are gone and the professor dusts his hands and strolls away as though nothing very unusual has occurred.

The next batch of bread is now ready and I shake my head. How can someone be so smart and also so stupid? In the case of the professor of know-everything, a bird in the hand is just as useless as two in the bush. I sigh, there will be no flavour of meat in tonight's offering.

I had almost forgotten the incident with the birds when some weeks later the professor puts up his hand to tell a story so that we might choose the dish our potatoes, turnips and cabbage would become that night.

That he should volunteer a story comes as a complete surprise. His demeanour on most nights is dismissive and, while he is not rude, it is easy to tell he is uninterested. Though with only the slightest encouragement he would expound one of his theories or explain how a steam train worked or a metal boat floated on water. He is not so much what you might call a storyteller as a fact-teller and seems totally uninterested in food.

As a matter of fact, the professor is the only one among us who appears perfectly content with the food I serve straight from The Family Frying Pan.

So when Professor Slotinowitz volunteers to tell us a story we don't quite know what to expect. Another of his endless theories perhaps? Or, at best, a hasty, tasteless meal cooked in a laboratory on a Bunsen burner while some pointless experiment occupied his mind which, when solved, will not put an extra crumb on his family table. That is, of course, if the professor ever had a family. It is difficult to imagine that the simple act of creation, the business of making a baby, could be grasped in a head so filled with theories, equations and scientific complexities.

'I was once the keeper of the Tsar's birds, of the Royal Aviary,' he begins, 'for I have always had a way with birds, a natural affinity, even if I say so myself.'

I nod, remembering the incident with the breakfast crumbs, though I can see that this information surprises the others.

'Perhaps you can catch us a brace of plump partridges for tomorrow night's dinner?' Mrs Olga Zorbatov quips. 'Partridge and Potato Pie served with a sweet Madeira wine.' She claps her hands to her breast, 'Oh my, oh my!'

The professor chooses to ignore this remark. 'As the Royal Ornithologist I was visited by bird salesmen from all over the world carrying cages of exotic birds. The great blue and yellow macaw, the exotic keel-billed toucan and the crimson topaz hummingbird from South America. The noisy pink and white galah, and parrots and rosellas of every colour from the Antipodes. From the Solomon Islands and German Guinea, the bird of paradise. Proud chickens with plumes as bright as peacocks and leg feathers of crimson and blue from China and regal peacocks themselves from the forests where tigers roam on the slopes of the Himalayas in the Kingdom of Nepal. Grey parrots from the Congo River in Africa which live for a hundred years, and blue doves from the spice island of Zanzibar. From the bitter soda lakes of German East Africa, the glorious lesser pink flamingo.

'Men of every colour and creed came to my door. Africans, black as polished ebony wood, with filed teeth and silver bangles banding their upper arms. Yellow-skinned Mongolians and shy, imperious, saffron-robed Tibetans, their eyes dark clove slits set in flat calm faces. Turbaned men from Afghanistan with fierce hooked noses and eyes as hard as tektites. Men from Bolivia, draped in brilliantly coloured blankets, who wore bowler hats and smoked thin cigars, which they held in slender coffee-coloured fingers.

'Enough, Professor!' Olga Zorbatov interrupts, 'Except for the chickens from China there is hardly a decent morsel in your grand aviary! I read once in a book that parrots tasted bitter as aloe oil and the peacock, when it is plucked of its fancy finery, is no more pleasure to eat than a common spatchcock taken from the pigeon loft.'

The professor is no Mr Mendelsohn and well used to interruption. Academics quarrel all the time and interjection is as common as spectacles to men of learning, so Mrs Z's comments are water off a duck's back.

'Tsar Nicholas took some pleasure in his aviary and I believe he thought it well worth the upkeep, which was considerable, but it was his daughter Princess Tatiana who loved to come each morning to see the birds.' The professor smiles. 'She was a pretty little creature with a brilliant musical ear and she would spend an hour or more each morning talking to the birds. She could emulate the exact tone, rhythm and intonation of every bird call in the great glass-domed Imperial Aviary. And repeat the honks and quacks of the geese, swans and wild duck which swam in the ponds and lakes created around it. She could as easily mimic the honk of the snow goose as she could the raucous squawking of a sulphur-crested cockatoo, and in the very next breath she might create the soft cooing of a blue dove or the call of the English nightingale. There seemed to be no bird call, no matter how strange, that didn't come to her ear naturally. She seemed quite capable of talking personally to the birds, which would flutter and dance excitedly in the air around her as she entered the aviary.

'To this remarkable talent Tatiana added another, an affinity with numbers, in this she was an equal genius.' The professor pauses, looking up at the stars, and then allows himself a sigh, 'If ever I should have had a child I would have wished it to be Tatiana, daughter of Tsar Nicholas. Indeed, I came to think of her in much these terms and could hardly wait for her to appear each morning when, after talking to the birds, she would take breakfast in the lodge with me. Here I gave her lessons in algebra and geometry and soon we moved into the realm of higher mathematics and abstract equations. What a delightful mind the child had and if Russia should ever have a queen, another Catherine the Great, it will be well served if they should choose the Princess Tatiana.'

'Ah, that is not likely, there is an heir at last, the continuity of the Romanoffs is now assured,' Olga Zorbatov says smugly.

I think to myself, We are all fleeing from the tyranny of Tsarist Russia and here is Mrs Z being a royalist, pompous as anything. Besides, she is interrupting too much and the professor's story is becoming really quite interesting.

'Is it true Prince Alexei has a rare blood disease and will not make old bones, perhaps not even grow to be an adult?' I ask. I heard this rumour from a monk who sold us a sack of potatoes at a monastery we had passed on our travels. He told me that one of their kind, a monk named Rasputin, had been selected by the Tsarina to be with the heir to the throne of all the Russias as his spiritual healer and that God had granted this monk the gift of stopping the boy from bleeding to death. I did not find this altogether strange, for it has been my observation that the Gentile God is very involved with blood in one way or another.

'It is quite true, the prince is a sickly child and often covered in bruises and there is a lot of loose talk, more than this I cannot tell you,' the professor says, before adding, 'Though I admit to having been told a little more in the utmost confidence.'

'Then it is true!' Olga Z says triumphantly, shaking her head up and down and pouting her lips. 'A queen for Russia, eh?'

'That is not what I said, Mrs Zorbatov, it was only a chance remark. Tatiana is a remarkable young lady, or was, until the Indian myna bird came into my life and completely spoiled our relationship.' The professor scratches his head and says ruefully, 'Now that I am gone from her life, one must suppose, she will be taught needlework and how, with good grace, to bear intolerably boring conversations.'

This last remark stops all the speculation about the condition of the Prince Alexei, heir to the Russian throne, and we all grow silent. The professor is about to get to the juicy bits.

The Indian myna bird is a most unprepossessing bird, not much bigger than twice the size of a sparrow with dull brown and pale yellow breast feathers, though it has a bright eye ringed with black and a lively, busy manner. It gives off the impression of intelligence as it cocks its head at human sounds and seems naturally curious. Easily tamed, it can be made to learn tricks and to emulate a number of expressions of the voice, so that there are those who believe that it can not only learn to speak but can understand what is being said as well. I must point out to you all that this is not true. The Indian myna, like the parrot, can learn sounds if they are constantly repeated, but has no comprehension of their meaning.

As I said before, it was the habit of the Princess Tatiana to take breakfast at my lodge, which also served as the gatehouse to the greater bird sanctuary. It was here that the bird salesmen with their exotic species would come. Princess Tatiana would often accompany me to the gate to look at the day's offerings. Sometimes she would urge me to purchase an exotic and beautiful specimen, and after I had carefully examined the bird to see that its feathers hadn't been dyed or new ones skilfully sewn to old with minute stitches or gummed to truncated quills, I might do so. But first I carefully questioned the salesman as to the bird's habitat so that we might place it within the great glass aviary where it was most likely to survive.

On the morning of the Indian myna bird, we had
been offered several fine specimens, including as I
recall a rufous-tailed jacamar from the tropical
rainforests of the Amazon, which I was obliged
reluctantly to refuse. It is a bird that lives mostly on
butterflies, and the butterfly house in the aviary
had for some reason, probably a malfunction of the
temperature, destroyed all this season's butterfly
pupae. The chances of our keeping the jacamar
alive through the winter were not very good, while
the price being asked for the exotic bird was not
inconsiderable. Despite the disappointment of the
princess I was forced to conclude that the Tsar's
money could be better spent elsewhere.

We had all but concluded our inspection of the
birds for sale that day when the princess stopped at an
enormous gilded cage beside which sat a most
imperious-looking man on a small carved stool. At
first appearance he seemed to be an Afghani, though
in some respects different. He had none of the
savage, bearded looks of his countrymen nor did he
have the ubiquitous rifle slung about his striped
ankle-length jalabi robe. Moreover, his face showed
not a single scar and while his nose was large and
carried the distinctive hook of his tribe, it was offset

by a neat moustache and a well-clipped goatee beard. And his hands were a contradiction, soft with his fingernails well manicured and rather long. He bowed his head respectfully when the Princess Tatiana approached, though he did not kneel and place his forehead on the ground, nor even did he rise.

I was first alerted to the situation when I heard the princess laugh and I looked up to see the large and, I must say, rather ostentatious cage. 'Look, Professor, a little brown bird of no value whatso-ever and even less charm in this big and silly cage,' she called out to me.

She had barely said this when I heard her laugh again, but as I could see her lips, I knew at once that this second laughter, so perfectly like her own, came from the small brown and yellow bird with black-ringed eyes and bright yellow legs which appeared a trifle too big for it.

The princess looked in surprise at the little bird then she clapped her hands, 'Oh, we must have it!' she exclaimed. 'You must buy this laughing bird at once, Professor.'

'It is not for sale,' the man seated beside the cage said quietly. His manner was not in the least imper-tinent, but he was definite in his resolve.

'Come now, my good man,' I said in somewhat of a superior tone, 'I am not so easily duped, the bird has no value but the cage is of silver, though I'll vouch there is too much lead in the mix. It is the cage you wish to sell, is it not?' I did not wait for his reply before continuing, 'Well, it is the bird we want and you may keep the gilded cage and sell it to some silly, degenerate nobleman of which Russia has far too many splendid examples.'

Tatiana giggled, the royal palace was constantly filled with slack-mouthed suitors from the nobility, some of whom would have great difficulty counting to the sum of their bejewelled fingers.

The Oriental ignored my rudeness. 'The bird is a gift from the Queen of Persia for the Princess Tatiana but it must be won by her in fair competition,' he said quietly.

'Competition? A gift to be won? Who will challenge Her Royal Highness?' I laughed at the indignity of the proposal, 'The Queen of Persia? And what in and what for?' I sniffed. 'The prize, a silly little brown bird?'

'The Indian myna bird is not a silly little brown bird and this one is bred of generations of Persian royal birds beginning in Asia Minor since time was an infant. It has an astonishing intelligence. The challenge will be at mathematics and bird calls!'

I must say I didn't like this arrogant and confident manner in the least but before I could protest the princess exclaimed, 'I should like that, I should like that very much indeed!' She turned to me, 'Professor, you must invite our new friend to breakfast in your lodge where the competition will take place. I shall order something nice for him from the kitchen, and you and I will have English porridge with honey as usual.'

'No, Princess,' the turbaned gentleman said quickly. 'The Queen of Persia has sent sweetmeats from the Orient. I will try this thing you call porridge and you must eat of our food, which I know will delight your palate.' He rose slowly and extended his hands to show a ruby ring on each forefinger with an Arabian script carved into the stone. 'I am the brother of the Sultan of Arabia, who also sends you greetings.'

It was plain to see that Tatiana was impressed, after all, it is not every day you meet the Sultan of Arabia's brother.

'We shall have to call the royal taster and your

governess and at least two referees, I shall be one and another must be found,' I said.

'By all means,' the sultan's brother said. 'Will you allow my servant to accompany me?'

We had barely noticed the presence of the bearded little man who had stood quietly some paces behind the sultan's brother.

'Certainly,' the princess said. 'He can also be the second referee if you like.'

The sultan's brother smiled. 'He is only a servant, Princess, he will carry the cage and then sit at my feet and sleep.'

The servant carried the great gilded cage into the lodge and set it up in the breakfast room behind a chair where the sultan's brother was invited to sit. Then, clasping his hands together as though in prayer, the servant bowed to us and took his place cross-legged at his master's feet, where he appeared almost instantly to fall asleep.

The royal taster and the governess were summonsed together with one of the royal accountants who had come to work early. Soon the table was covered with the most exotic food. Chocolates and Turkish delight and all manner of dried fruits and nuts and little sweet cakes, all of this supplied from a great bag the sultan's brother's servant had given to my servant. Wine was brought for the adults though the sultan's brother asked only for water with a little juice of the lemon added.

A plate of steaming porridge was brought for him along with a goblet of water. He dipped a spoon into the porridge and then lifted it to his imperious nose and sniffed. 'No smell? Perhaps just a hint of honey?' Then he tasted it, though very tentatively, on the tip of his pink tongue. He pulled a face, more a polite grimace, and then placed his spoon down. 'I have already eaten,' he said, handing the plate back to a servant to take away. He waved his hand across the table filled with eastern delights. 'Eat, please. Enjoy, compliments of the Queen of Persia.'

I'm not at all sure I was pleased about the way he was taking over and I must admit it was a very strange breakfast. But the princess seemed happy enough and seemed to relish all sorts of delicious bits and pieces and soon declared herself wonderfully satisfied even though the royal taster looked decidedly sick from the overly rich food.

'Now for the competition, Sultan's Brother,' Tatiana said. 'How do the rules go?'

'No rules, just sounds and numbers. You may

keep the Indian myna bird if you can make a bird sound with your throat or make up a mathematical calculation it cannot repeat exactly or answer accurately.'

I must admit I laughed out loud. 'Sir, your bird is soon lost.'

'Shall we make a wager on that?' the sultan's brother offered gently.

We all laughed. 'You do not know what you are saying, sir, the princess is gifted in emulating the song of birds and also in mathematics. Besides, we are servants of the Tsar and cannot wager money on his daughter.'

'Oh, but I can!' Princess Tatiana cried. She turned to the young clerk. 'I have money of my own, money sent to me by Queen Victoria and other money, have I not?'

The accountant nodded his head glumly, not at all sure that he was authorised to make expenditure on behalf of the young princess.

'Good! Then, Professor, you shall wager for me!'

The sultan's brother reached for a leather bag somewhere in his striped robes and counted ten English gold sovereigns onto the table. 'Shall we start with only a small wager? I do not wish to embarrass the princess.'

I looked at the ten gold coins in dismay. 'I do not have the authority!' I stammered.

'Yes, you have, I just gave it to you,' Tatiana cried. 'Let's get on with it please, Professor.'

'I only have the Tsar's money, which I use for the purchase of birds,' I said helplessly.

'The fifteen-year-old princess sighed and clucked her tongue. 'You will be repaid every kopek should I lose, which I shall not.' She turned to the sultan's brother. 'Shall we begin? What bird call shall I make, Professor?'

I placed ten gold coins on the table to the value of the English sovereigns. 'The Common Potoo, *Nyctibius griseus*,' I replied. This strange relative of the nightjar can be heard on any moonlit night and comes from tropical South America. It has a most difficult to emulate warble of several notes, as though three or four different birds are in harmony, and it was one of the bird calls Tatiana found at first most difficult.

Almost at once the strange, plaintive cry of this ugly little bird which, as a matter of interest, has the additional ability to distort its body so that it might appear to be a part of a log or a wayside stone, came from the princess. It was well delivered and those around the breakfast table who heard it smiled, as it was indeed a most complex call.

Our smiles were almost instantly wiped from our faces, for Tatiana had barely drawn breath again when a precise emulation of the sound came from the myna bird. My ear for birdsong is perfect and both the princess and I knew that we had lost our wager.

The sultan's brother added my coins to the pile in front of him, 'Shall we wager double your last bet on the next call?'

'Yes, yes, the English nightingale, a complete stanza!' the princess exclaimed, clapping her hands gleefully.

Almost immediately she started to sing in the beautiful call of the nightingale. It was an enchanting sound and masterful in its rendition, and brought tears to the eyes of those who listened. But no sooner was it over than the little myna bird repeated it as perfectly as she had rendered it. The sultan's brother raised his eyebrows at me and I was forced to nod, then he took the twenty gold coins from my side of the table and added them to the pile in front of him.

'No more!' I cried. 'We have seen enough. You may take your myna bird away with you. We do not need a bird who can sing like all the other birds, we have a Russian princess who can do that!'

Tatiana looked dismayed. 'But we have hardly begun, Professor!'

'Princess, we have lost thirty gold coins, not quite a king's ransom, but the better part of my monthly budget for buying birds.'

'But I told you, Papa will pay! I have my own money, we haven't challenged the bird to any maths!'

'Shall we say sixty gold coins, double what you have already bet?' the Oriental man, whom I was beginning greatly to dislike, suggested. My heart beat faster as I observed the pile of gold coins on the table in front of him. To add sixty more would take my entire budget for the summer.

'No, no, I really must refuse.' I looked for help from the accountant but he avoided my eyes and, turning his back on me, reached over for a piece of Turkish delight.

'Oh, just one more, please, Professor, just one truly hard one.'

The sultan's brother's hand rose. 'The rules for

mathematics are different. I will give you a problem and then you will compete with the bird to see who can most quickly solve it.' He pointed to me. 'So that there is no suggestion of prior knowledge, that is to say, the bird has already been taught the answer, you, Professor, shall set the second problem.'

I shrugged my shoulders and counted out sixty gold coins from the velvet bag on my lap, and when I had laid them before me I knew that only two more coins sat in the bottom of the bag. I had spent four years' salary for a mathematics professor at the Moscow Academy where I had once taught.

'Sixteen multiplied by 29.5, divided by 11.5, subtract six and multiply by 77,' the sultan's brother announced.

It was child's play. If this was the sort of maths the myna bird could do we would win all our money back and all that of the odious Oriental. Tatiana would make short work of such a problem, in thirty seconds or less. The seconds ticked by and the bird hopped in what appeared to be some agitation from one perch to another. 'Two thousand, six hundred and ninety-eight point three four, do you wish the continuing fractions?' the princess shouted triumphantly.

'The princess is very clever,' the sultan's brother

said quietly and pushed all the coins back over to my side of the table. I must say I was profoundly relieved. Princess Tatiana was capable of much better and it was my turn to create a complex equation. 'Shall it be double again?' I asked, looking at the one hundred and twenty gold coins in front of me.

'Of course,' the Oriental said, though I thought with a little less enthusiasm.

I set a new problem much more difficult than the one set by the sultan's brother, in fact, one which was at the extreme limit of Tatiana's capacity. It would take her two minutes or more of mental calculations and I sat back to wait, thinking of the fortune we were about to earn. But in less than twenty seconds the bird had the answer, which, by the way, was far less than I would have required to calculate the answer to such a problem myself.

The sultan's brother rose from his chair and leaned over and drew the golden coins over to his side of the table and swept them into a leather satchel. 'There is a matter of one hundred and twenty gold coins to come from you, Professor,' he said quietly.

'I cannot pay you now, you will have to take a promissory note.'

I turned to the accountant, who shrugged and

wrote out the note, insisting that I authorise it with my signature.

'Thank you,' the sultan's brother said. He rose from the table and kicked the servant who lay asleep at his feet. The little man seemed to wake up with a start and scrambled to his feet and from his pocket took a handful of corn which he scattered on the floor of the cage. Then he stood to rigid attention beside the gilded cage as the Indian myna bird pecked busily at the granules of corn. The sultan's brother bowed to us all, last of all to Princess Tatiana.

'You have been most hospitable and I thank you. As a token of my esteem and that of the Queen of Persia you may ask the royal myna bird any question you like about your own future, for, in addition to its other talents, the bird possesses the gift of prophecy as well.'

'Please, we have had enough, I must ask you to leave at once,' I said sternly.

The sultan's brother looked down his imperious nose at me. 'Be calm, Professor, there is no wager involved in this.'

'Any question?' the princess asked excitedly, she seemed not in the least concerned at losing so much money.

The sultan's brother nodded.

'About the future?'

Again the sultan's brother agreed.

'Will I grow up and meet a handsome prince and live happily ever after?' Princess Tatiana asked.

We all looked to the bird, which had suddenly and in great agitation flown up to its perch and commenced to chirp in the familiar and not very pleasant manner of an Indian myna bird. The chirping grew most agitated but it was no more than that, the chirp of an Indian myna bird, and not a single vowel or consonant that might be mistaken for a human language escaped from its beak as an answer to the question the princess had asked. Then it did a last frantic flutter and dropped dead, falling off its perch to the bottom of the cage, its over-large yellow legs pointing straight upwards.

'A terrible omen!' Mrs Zorbatov exclaims. 'It dropped dead, the bird died, can't you see? It *is* the prophecy, the Princess Tatiana is going to die!'

We all look at each other in horror. While we have no time for the Tsar, me least of all with my whole village destroyed and my people killed by his Cossacks, we nevertheless wish no harm on the beautiful Princess Tatiana, who seems to us the first intelligent Russian royal since Peter the Great.

'That was some bird!' I say at last. 'Some schmarty-pants bird!'

The professor shakes his head. 'It wasn't the myna bird who was smart, it was the professor who was stupid! You see it was the Oriental gentleman's servant, he was the smart one, a brilliant mimic and, as well, a ventriloquist not to mention a mathematical genius.'

'Oh yeah? Well what about the bird dropping dead like that, then?' Olga Zorbatov challenges. Like all of us she wants the Indian myna bird to stay smart so the story won't lose its mystery.

The professor sighs. 'The corn was poisoned, the corn the servant threw into the bottom of the cage killed the bird.'

The remainder of the story I shall tell, for it was the reason the professor was included into our group of refugees fleeing from the Tsar's secret police.

Like most young women, the princess had become over-excited at the prospect of the competition and when the professor visited the royal exchequer to claim the money she had promised his request was promptly denied, and he was confronted with the promissory note he had signed. When the young accountant and all the other witnesses were called in, they, for fear of becoming implicated, denied that the princess had agreed that the money be used for gambling purposes and that she would repay it from her own pocket. As for the princess herself, she simply wasn't asked if she had authorised the professor to act as he did. Despite his pleas for her to appear on his behalf, this too was denied to him.

The professor was arrested and thrown into jail for the fraudulent use of the Tsar's money. He was sentenced to twenty years in Siberia but escaped from the train taking him there when a guard shook him awake in the early hours of the morning. The engine had stopped to take on water. 'Go,' the guard whispered, pushing the professor off the train, 'the Princess Tatiana can do no more than this for you, if you are caught you will be immediately shot!'

Little did we know as we sat around the fire that night that not many years later the Tsar and the Tsarina, Prince Alexei, the haemophiliac heir to the throne, the Princess Tatiana and her four sisters would all be shot, murdered by the Reds in the 1917 Russian Revolution.

Maybe the corn was poisoned, maybe not. Maybe by dropping dead, that clever Indian myna bird was trying to tell the Princess Tatiana something after all?

THE BANQUET OF
PAST SUFFERING AND
FUTURE JOY

Olga Zorbatov is a seamstress, or so she says, though she has not been observed with so much as a needle and thread in her possession since coming to us.

Her only interests seem to be in matters both gastronomical and verbal, for she is constantly preoccupied with food and chatter. She is also most contrary; no matter what one says, Mrs Z feels compelled to take the opposite viewpoint.

If we are fortunate enough to have sufficient beetroot to make a nice borscht soup and someone observes that it is lacking in a little salt, then Mrs Z will immediately declare it to be too salty for her taste.

She has grown quite thin, which is only a manner of speaking for she is still a big woman but much trimmed down and even more healthy than when she first joined our group.

How very fat she was at that time, with double and even treble chins. A person shouldn't call another person fat, that is, if such a thing can be avoided, but with Olga Zorbatov, believe me, fat was a compliment compared to what she was. She would wobble like a great jelly as she walked and we all feared she would slow us down, for she had the greatest trouble keeping up and often lagged behind the professor who uses a walking stick and suffers from arthritis in his hip.

But she is not without courage and, besides, she has a strange gift. She is a remarkable scavenger and, most days, seems able to prophesy where a little food may be found. Quite how she does this is a mystery and we are often forced to shake our heads in amazement.

We will be travelling on the road and in the distance and to our left might be the dark line of a pine forest. Mrs Z will stop suddenly as though she is sniffing the air.

'Mushrooms!' she will announce. Then she will

turn to the children. 'Take a big basket, look carefully under the trunks of the larger trees, brush
away the dead pine needles, you'll find them
there.'

If our resident mushroom expert, Anya Mendelsohn, is feeding her baby and won't accompany
them, the children will go reluctantly, kicking at
stones and looking back over their shoulders. Kids
do not like entering dark woods and there is always
something scary about a pine forest. But sure
enough, they will return in an hour or two with
much excitement and present me with a basket
brimful of wild mushrooms.

That is the strange thing. She seems to know in
the morning before we set out whether there will be
extra food to find during the day's long journey.
She will point in a direction when we are all ready
to set out for the day, and we know now to obey
even if the path seems at first to be quite wrong.
Soon enough we'll come to a wayside apple
orchard with windblown fruit scattered under the
trees.

Or she might point to a swamp and say, 'Goose
eggs!' and the children will scamper off and return
several minutes later with a clutch of large eggs.

Occasionally she'll point to a green waterhole in a river almost dried up in the summer heat. 'Fish over there and biting!' she will announce. Sure enough, Mr Petrov, the blacksmith, who is the resident fisherman, will soon land a fat carp or two for our dinner.

It is quite uncanny, especially as Mrs Z knows nothing of country matters and can't tell a farm goose from a Moscovy duck unless it is already plucked and dressed by the butcher. I once asked her how she came to have this second sight for the whereabouts of food, which I must point out she lacks in everything else and is much more likely to rush in like a bull in a china shop than to be in the least sensitive to the feelings of the others.

'I see it in the stars,' she said. Seeing my bemused expression, she continued. 'Since the death of my husband, God rest his soul, I sleep little at night.' This was true enough, I would often wake in the night to find her walking about, muttering away and gesticulating to the night sky. 'I watch the sky and speak to my husband, Sergei, who tells me in what direction we must travel in the morning to find a morsel to eat.' Mrs Z looked at me, one eyebrow slightly raised. 'Last night Sergei was riding on the tail of Pisces and today Mr Petrov caught three fat fish!'

I have mentioned before that it is best to mind your own business when you are travelling with others and so I nodded my head as though this revelation was a perfectly satisfactory explanation. I may be a country girl but I am not stupid. If Mrs Z is a little soft in the head what does it matter? Who am I to question her astral conversations with her dead husband? Why should I care if he has his head stuck in the jaws of Leo the Lion, or rides on the tail of Pisces the Fish when the results are of such benefit to all of us? So I keep my mouth shut and say nothing to the others because now I know Olga Z is definitely crazy.

So when she put up her hand to tell a story, given her passion for food and her verbal dexterity, her astral connections and her lively imagination, crazy or not, I anticipated a star performance. Little did I know how right I would be, though none of us could have suspected the strange tale she was about to tell.

This is Olga Zorbatov's story as told to us under the stars somewhere in Russia.

. . .

'There are many ways to use an astrological chart,' she begins, 'and almost all have to do with personality. We are all born under an astrological sign and there are some people who believe that we are trapped within our signs. I presume all of you know nothing about astrology?' She gives the professor a scathing look, 'Although the professor is bound to think he knows it all!'

Professor Slotinowitz shrugs, 'Astronomy, my dear, a little. Of the witchcraft of astrology, I know nothing,' he says in a mild and pleasant voice. I must say the professor is learning a lot in human relations, before he would have walked out for sure.

Mrs Z gives him a malevolent look but, thank God, does not choose to quarrel with him and continues with her story. 'Allow me to explain. The child born under the Leo on the Zodiac chart is said to be a natural leader. Someone born under the Scorpio sign is thought to have a sharp tongue and a peremptory manner. Taurus the Bull makes for one impetuous and unthinking, likely to tramp over people's feelings. If you are born under the sign of Aries the Ram . . .' Mrs Z pauses and looks a trifle embarrassed, 'you are said to be good in the bedchamber.'

This brings laughter from all of us. Then Mr

Petrov, the blacksmith, who is responsible for the fine fish stew we are going to enjoy tonight, asks Mrs Z if she was born under the sign of Taurus.

'How did you guess?' she says, plainly surprised. Mrs Z seems confused when her remark causes a gale of laughter.

Olga Zorbatov continues. 'Now this would be very well if it worked, but how often do we find a Leo person as timid as a mouse and quite unable to make a decision? And a Scorpio who is completely unselfish and lives to be in the service of others? Or a Taurus like myself who is not in the least clumsy and by nature sensitive? Do you get the idea?'

We all nod our heads.

'Well, this apparent contradiction worried my husband, Sergei, who was a cook and also an astrologer with a growing reputation. "Olga, sweetheart?" he said to me one night as we dined on the roof of our small house at midnight under the stars. You see, he would come home late from where he worked as head chef in the kitchen of the Hotel Grande Rex in Moscow, which, as you must all know, is where only the highest of the Russian nobility wish to be seen dining. He would return home late from the steaming atmosphere of the great kitchen and want to partake of a meal at midnight in the open air under the stars. Though, of course, this was only possible in the summer.

'"Yes, my beloved, what is it?" I replied.

'"Look!" Sergei said. "How brightly Taurus the Bull shines tonight."

'I spread goose pâté on a small slice of fresh soda bread and poured vodka into the silver horn he loved to use as his goblet and handed both to him. "It burns bright for you, my beautiful husband," I said.'

'Taurus is never overly bright in the Moscow sky,' the professor says suddenly.

'So now already the Birdman of St Petersburg is telling this story?' Olga Z asks, appealing to all of us.

'On that particular night it burned bright, Professor!' I interject hurriedly.

'So, let me continue.' Mrs Z turns to the professor. 'With your permission, of course, Professor-of-little-brown-birds-that-make-a-fool-of-so-called-smart-men!'

'We must have no more interruptions, please!' I say sternly, using authority I don't really have.

'Thank you, Mrs Moses,' Olga Zorbatov says. 'It is nice to know there is somebody civilised

here! If you remember before I was so rudely interrupted, my husband was about to speak.'

'Olga, sweetheart, I have a theory that heaven is the
great kitchen of human possibilities, and that the
stars are the cooking ingredients and the signs of
the Zodiac are the dishes of the personality. We
astrologers have it all wrong, people are not
trapped within their astrological signs, it is rather
more likely that if we are born under a sign that we
can use the characteristics of that sign to effect
good or evil on others. A Leo, for instance, can
teach his children the principles of leadership,
which is good, or he can be so adamant about being
the leader that he can cow his family and rob them
of initiative forever, which is bad. For instance,
you, who are gentle as a lamb, are born under the
sign of Taurus the Bull, but you do not choose to be
impetuous and unthinking, which is bad, but stead-
fast, loyal and protective, which is good.'

As he finished speaking, I picked out a *gozin-
nakh* from a small silver platter and popped it into
Sergei's mouth. This small ball-shaped confection,
you will all know of course, is made entirely of
chopped nuts, honey and sugar. 'You are so very

clever, Sergei, when did you come upon this brilliant theory that the heavens are the great kitchen of human possibilities?'

'By watching people eat. There is a saying among chefs that people are the food they eat. Watch what people eat and you will at once know a great deal about them.'

'And what does this have to do with the stars?'

'Simple, if you change what they eat, you change what they are! If a woman has been completely dominated by her husband who is a Leo, the meat eater, she will be forced to eat too much meat and her diet must be immediately adjusted, because every time she eats meat she will feel much burdened by her husband's personality.'

Even a stupid country woman like myself can see that there are several holes in this astrological argument and I can hear the professor snorting in indignation to himself. But we dare not interrupt for fear of upsetting Mrs Z further and this theory of her husband's makes some sort of crazy sense, if you know what I mean.

Mrs Z continues on with her story.

. . .

Sergei was born under the sign of Sagittarius the Archer and was therefore obsessive and single-minded and always aimed straight at the target of his particular ambition. Taking our modest savings, he opened a small sanatorium which was centred around a magnificent kitchen. He let it be known among the noble customers of the Hotel Grande Rex that, through the practice of astrological dietary discipline, he could change difficult personalities for the better and also cure depression, aggression, fits, ravings, suicidal tendencies, loss of memory, uncontrolled weeping, coarse language in women and all the various moods and mental frustrations and aberrations commonly found in persons of noble lineage.

The nobility were only too pleased to find somewhere to dump their misfits and in no time Dr Zorbatov, Professor of Astrological Science and Zodiac Law, the title Sergei gave to himself, found he had more patients than he could handle. Princes, grand dukes, generals and counts paid huge sums just to gain a few places nearer the top of the waiting list. It seemed that in every aristocratic Russian family there were more than a few members in need of the good professor's astrological diet and personality adjustment.

· · ·

'Fifteen years I studied at the Moscow Academy to become a professor and this astrological charlatan helps himself!' Professor Slotinowitz mumbles in disgust behind me. Thank heaven, Mrs Z doesn't hear him, or appears not to anyway, for she keeps talking:

The curious thing was that it appeared to work. If not in every case, some patients had lost too many marbles too long ago for anything to be done, but in a great many situations.

Sergei worked out an astrological dietary regime for each patient, but only after having cast an astrological chart of the patient upon admission and from this, taken together with a great deal of close questioning about the patient's family and family history, he determined what they should eat. He had a vast knowledge of food and herbs and the effect various cuisines have on the human body and mind and he used this to great effect.

Often the patients would enter the sanatorium in poor health and in a few weeks or months they would be different people, their symptoms eliminated. Those who had entered fat and flaccid would leave with a trim waist and in the best of health.

My clever Sergei also came up with what he

called his 'patient dialogue' and as the sanatorium grew larger he employed people from the academy who were studying the new science of the mind to listen to the patients and to make notes as they spoke of their past lives. Soon they would uncover a history of early beatings or cruelty or, as was often enough the case with his female patients – though not always were they women – sexual abuse from a father or an uncle or even an older cousin. And it was from these sessions that he invented his master therapy, the Banquet of Past Suffering and Future Joy.

This was a grand affair, a banquet to which the patients were required to invite themselves when they felt ready. If they volunteered, believing themselves sufficiently recovered to undergo the routine, they were counselled as to the nature of the dishes available to be eaten. There were twelve dishes in all and they were divided into six 'good' dishes and six 'bad' dishes, each of the twelve corresponding to a sign in the Zodiac.

Each dish symbolised a personality characteristic which could be associated with the astrological sign it came under, or rather, it was a symbol for that characteristic. As I have previously said,

Sergei believed that there were good and bad aspects of every star sign, but for the purposes of his banquet dishes, the bad dishes represented the worst aspect of its sign and the good dishes the best aspect to be found under its particular star.

There was the Aries Pie, a dish made of mutton and in particular from the meat of a ram. This pie represented the sexual drive gone wrong and sexual abuse of a small child.

Then there was a huge beef steak that was named the Tyrant Taurus, which represented the bully and the tyrant.

Then came a chicken soup which, strangely enough, represented Scorpio, the sign of the scorpion, for while it tasted delicious, after a few spoonfuls it became apparent that it was extremely hot, laced with fiery red peppers so that the tongue swelled in the mouth. This dish stood for temper and subsequent beatings, love promised and then withdrawn, duplicity and betrayal.

The Coil of Cancer was a length of sausage a metre long that lay coiled like a snake upon a white plate and was filled with every imaginable flavour given to sausages. It represented mysterious stomach pains, headaches, temporary blindness, uncontrollable temper tantrums, depression and other mental maladies which lacked a ready explanation.

Under the sign of Leo was a dish of raw meat thinly sliced and seasoned with herbs, pepper and capers and served with hot English mustard. It stood for undue severity and unreasonable control and the demand for unquestioning and absolute obedience.

Finally, on the list of negative characteristic dishes, came the Capricorn Stew, a dish which took after the goat it represented. In fact, it was made of goat's meat but as the goat is known to eat anything, it contained just about everything you could imagine could safely be contained in a concoction cooked in the juices of meat and vegetables. Capricorn Stew represented any past and negative afflictions visited upon the patient which he or she had not yet discovered or spoken about.

These six bad characteristic dishes were collectively known as the Food of Sorrow.

Then there were the astrological dishes which contained positive characteristics, those personal traits to which most humans aspire. These were known as the Food of Joy.

The Gemini twins were represented by a wonderful dessert known as Gemini Gloriana, a dish exquisitely sweet to the taste but with an occasional spoonful taken distinctly tart. It represented a natural easygoing personality, not easily upset, but if given a just cause not incapable of responding.

Virgo the Virgin was a lemon sorbet, delightfully fresh tasting and clean to the palate. The characteristics it represented were openness and innocence.

Aquarius, the water symbol, may at first have seemed a fairly dull dish, but at the banquet it proved to be a most popular addition. It was simply a large crystal jug of pure spring water with a tincture of various oriental herbs added. It represented vigour, decency, sobriety and good health. Aquarius was also represented by a bowl of fresh fruit and the additional characteristic this added was a sweetness of disposition.

Pisces was a salmon pâté, extremely subtle to the taste, and it represented the salmon who swims for so long against the stream and so stood for individuality, determination and character.

Sagittarius was not a dish but a clear, white wine with a most beguiling bouquet and a clean, delicious flavour. While it seemed bland enough, a single mouthful went straight to the blood to produce an invigorating effect which turned easily into laughter. The characteristic it represented need hardly be explained, it represented constant good humour.

Finally there was Libra, the scales, a most popular dish for it was not a dish at all but a pair of scales which allowed any of the guests to take equal amounts of any two dishes so that they weighed precisely the same. This allowed for a mix of positive characteristics. For instance a hundred grams of lemon sorbet taken with a fresh pear promised a sweet disposition and a charming and innocent nature, a combination much liked by the female guests at the banquet. Many of the men, however, chose two dishes which taken together would result in a well-balanced personality.

All this talk of food, even the kind that represented the bad characteristics, was making us exceedingly hungry and the fish soup I had made from the fish Mrs Z had second-sighted and Mr Petrov had caught was smelling delicious. It was time Olga Zorbatov concluded her story or we would all soon be completely famished, though how her story would end was a complete mystery and she had, in my mind anyway, already received very high marks for storytelling.

Well, now that you know the dishes served at the Banquet of Past Suffering and Future Joy, it remains only for me to explain the procedure.

On the afternoon before the banquet the patients were taken into a small garden known as the Garden of Forgotten Sorrows, which led off from the banquet hall. Here they were given a silver spade and made to dig a hole the depth of their arm and then a little more, so that by reaching into it they were unable to touch the bottom. Though the soil was soft enough and easy to dig, most of the patients had never handled a spade in their lives before and took to the task with little expertise. But, despite their grumbling, they were not allowed to hand the job over to a servant as it was compulsory to complete the task themselves. The soil from the hole was then neatly piled beside it and the patient's name placed on a small paper flag which was stuck on top of the pile.

The banquet took place under glittering crystal chandeliers with all the trappings usual to a grand and important occasion. Musicians played from the more famous of the Russian, French and Italian composers, though the Germans, out of favour with the Tsar, were not represented. There were jugglers and acrobats and exotic dancers and, at one stage, a full military band marched through the hall playing a march which celebrated the defeat of the British and French in the Crimea.

Guests were dressed in all their finery, in uniforms and evening dress, the men with full decorations worn, and the women emblazoned with diamonds and pearls and glittering tiaras. At nine o'clock the dancing stopped. The patients/guests sat down to eat and the first astrological dish of their personal choice, the dish of negativity, was placed before each of them.

Dr Sergei Zorbatov, Professor of Astrological Science and Zodiac Law, addressed the glittering throng. By now he was an immensely rich and powerful man with friends in high places, the confidant of grand dukes, counts, generals and politicians. In a few short years he had brought more sanity into the Russian nobility than had existed for the past four hundred years. There was even talk that the Tsar would make him Minister for Culture.

'You will eat every morsel set before you, not one crumb, not one spoonful must be left of the dish you choose. This is an order!'

There was a loud groan from the assembled guests, the food set in front of them was more even than a starving peasant could hope to eat in a week in paradise. But such was the authority and esteem in which they held Sergei Zorbatov, who had brought most of them in touch with reality for the first time in their lives, that they simply bowed their heads and started to eat the first of the negativity dishes they had chosen.

They ate until they could eat no more, whereupon one of the observers allocated to watch, judging the time was right, would place a bib over the head of a satiated banqueter and lead him quickly to the Garden of Forgotten Suffering, where he was made to stand beside the hole he had previously dug and marked with his title and name.

As each patient appeared in the garden, looking much the worse for wear, the professor would address him by his name and title. For example, he might say, 'Prince Nicolae Dimitri Pyotr Tolstoy, you are here to be granted complete and unconditional absolution from your past, you are now forever rid of your guilt and as a demonstration of this the harm done to you and the guilt you feel will be buried, forever expelled from your body and your soul.'

A servant would then hand the prince a small crystal goblet of clear liquid which he would suppose to be vodka, but was in fact a potion made from the castor-oil plant. The prince, at Sergei's command to drink, would throw back his head and down the contents of the glass. Almost instantly he would buckle over and a moment later he would vomit every morsel of the negative astrological dish into the hole in front of him, spitting the last of the evil out of his mouth. Then he would be made to kneel and scoop up the soil and fill in the hole, in this way burying the past with his own hands.

When this task of absolution and renewal was completed, a servant would bring him a bowl of warm water and a towel and he was allowed to wash his face and hands. Whereupon he was given a goblet of Sagittarius wine, the wine of invigoration and pleasant humour, and led back into the banquet hall where he would be placed at a second table with fresh linen, crystal and silver, and presented with the astrological dishes of future sanity and peace of mind.

Olga Zorbatov looks up and shrugs her shoulders. 'That is my story,' she says simply. Then, turning to me, she announces, 'Mrs Moses, the astrological fish we are eating tonight in the form of a stew smells delicious and I, for one, am starved.'

As usual it remains for me to complete the story and it was several weeks before I could pluck up the courage to approach Mrs Z. I would wake up during the night to find her wandering about talking to her husband, who, it seemed, continued to gambol around the Zodiac, for she had lost none of her second-sight since the night of the story and we still depended on her to find that little extra to make our journey bearable and keep us from starvation.

One night I awoke, it was a full moon and almost light enough to read a book. At first I heard and then moments later saw Mrs Z talking to the sky. I had seen this often enough before but quite why I decided this time to approach her I cannot say. I rose from my blanket beside the fire and, walking over, tapped her on the shoulder and said, 'Excuse me, Mrs Z, is there anything I can do for you?'

She turned slowly, as though she was in a trance. 'You want to know what happened to my husband, don't you, Mrs Moses?'

I nodded, too confounded to find the words.

'He was murdered.'

My hand went to my throat. 'Oh, how sad! Was it one of the people who attended his sanatorium?'

'No, Mrs Moses, he was killed by a lonely and bitter woman who, every night for a thousand nights and more, waited on the roof, under the stars, for her husband. Each night she prepared a midnight feast for him consisting of the most delectable dishes and chilled a bottle of the finest vodka to drink from the silver horn he had once so loved.

'But her husband was too busy dining with dukes and sleeping with countesses and he had no more time to meet the woman under the stars.' Mrs Z sighed. 'So the woman ate the entire midnight feast by herself and grew very fat and cried herself to sleep every night. And then one night he came to the roof. I think he came to tell her that he was leaving her. But first he stood with his hands clasped behind his back and watched the stars and then he spoke.

'"Look, Olga, there is Taurus the Bull," he pointed to the night sky. "It is your sign."

'For a moment the woman's heart leapt and she took the silver horn and filled it with vodka and started to walk towards him, to forgive him. Her husband had come back to her and it would be like old times.

'Then he said, "I don't suppose you can help being fat and ugly and clumsy, as bulls are naturally all of these unpleasant things." He turned around to face her. "My dear, I do not love you any more and have come to take my leave of you."

'It was then that Olga Zorbatov charged him and knocked him down and stabbed him through the heart with the silver horn. What else could she do? She was born under the sign of Taurus and she behaved in the only way a bull knows how when it is baited beyond endurance.'

THE BLACKSMITH WITH
A BELUGA TONGUE

M_r Petrov likes to call himself a practical man and when folk ask him what he does he shrugs his shoulders. 'I am a blacksmith,' he says without pride and then adds self-deprecatingly, 'I put shoes on horses and fix handles onto cooking pots.' He once picked up The Family Frying Pan and held it in his large fist as though judging its weight and quality and for once the old frying pan did not look too big for its boots! He grinned. 'A fine pan, Mrs Moses, the very best, solid as a blacksmith's head.'

I'm not sure what we would do without Mr Petrov, for amongst such a bunch of misfits a practical man is badly needed. He can mend shoes, catch fish, cut firewood, trap small animals and birds, build a rope bridge across a rushing stream and make a snug shelter from bark and twigs and stuff just lying around. While this one argues with that one about how a project should be undertaken, Mr Petrov goes quietly ahead and before you know it we are saved once again from disaster.

Like Mr Mendelsohn, Mr Petrov is not a big talker and, again, both men have beautiful hands, one for the violin and the other for mending things. The musician's hands are slim and elegant, soft as a girl's from the city, with the fingers seemingly too long, kept clean and white with the nails neatly trimmed. And the blacksmith's are broad and blunt and square, powerful hands with the nails broken and the palms callused so that when he shakes your hand your fist disappears completely and you hope he won't squeeze it too hard. But, big as they are, that never happens because Mr Petrov has a gentle touch.

One night when Mr Petrov said quietly that it was time he told a story to enhance the evening meal (the usual *melange* of turnips, beets and a potato or two), we were all delighted. Though, I must say, I for one didn't expect much of a story but the mere fact that Mr P wanted to join in the storytelling was a delight to us all.

Practical people get on with things and it is my experience that they seldom embroider a point or are in the least romantic, so while we were pleased that he was coming out of his shell, we were not exactly holding our breath for an earth-shattering debut.

'I was born in a small fishing village,' Mr Petrov begins, 'on the banks of the Volga River. Its name is not important, there are twenty villages along our stretch of the shoreline and each is no more distinguished than the other. The fishing rights to a stretch of the great river were decided in ancient times and must be strictly observed, and the life of a river fisherman is very hard. Sometimes the fish disappear for weeks and the greatest prize, the noble sturgeon, may not choose to use your stretch of the shoreline for years. My family were poor and like most Volga fishermen always in debt to the caviar buyers from St Petersburg, Moscow and Persia, and so they were determined that I, their only son, Petrov Petrovitch would enjoy a less precarious vocation.'

'You are an only child? I too am an only child!'

Pretty Miss Tamara Polyansky exclaims in a surprised voice, as though being an only child was some sort of miracle to be marvelled at instead of only something moderately rare.

'Shush, Tamara!' Olga Zorbatov says, as usual without a hint of good manners. Though for once we are all rather pleased, none of us want Mr Petrov to dry up from a sudden fit of nerves. Anyway, Tamara Polyansky is a 'Miss Showbiz' and once she gets started nothing can stop her gabbing on about acrobats and high-wire acts and dashing young men in very tight tights. *Oi Vey!* I should be so lucky! But this was no time for daydreaming or showbiz talk!

'I have five sisters,' Mr Petrov says quietly, 'and so being a boy and the youngest I was spoiled by them all.' He laughs and then proceeds with his tale.

Nothing but being a blacksmith was good enough for me. A blacksmith's living does not depend on the widow-making sea or the unreliable coming of the sturgeon.

Once every ten years this may happen on your particular shore and then there is a killing for the village. But the occasional taking of the caviar, the roe of the sturgeon fish, is only sufficient to keep poor men still poor after they have paid their debts to the caviar buyers, bought new nets, a boat or a donkey engine and repaired the roof of their cottage and put aside a little for a daughter's dowry.

It is the middle men who grow rich. The caviar merchants and dealers from Moscow and St Petersburg and the dark-eyed men who arrive in the season from Persia. They all wear gold and diamond rings, shiny boots that reach to their fat knees and fine woollen coats that carelessly sweep the ground. Their hands are soft and their tongues oily and they can steal the nose off an honest fisherman's face without him knowing about it until he tries to sniff.

And so I was apprenticed to a blacksmith, a trade known to be consistent. It was work I was well suited to do, for, while I was big and clumsy on the small fishing boats, I was well suited to the hammer and tongs. I took to the furnace and anvil with alacrity and did not miss the water too much. The blacksmith shop was thankfully situated near the riverbank. I could look out and see the boats returning in the late afternoon and see the ebb and flow of the mother of all rivers and witness the rhythm and the changing of the seasons, and not lose touch with the generations of family who had served and worked the Volga.

You see, we have been fisherfolk since time out of mind, maybe for a thousand years, maybe more. Each year we pray to Saint Peter the Fisherman and ask that he direct the sturgeon to our part of the river, but sturgeon are unpredictable and we are lucky if they should come once in three years. In the meantime we fish for less exotic fare and hope that we might catch enough in our nets to feed our families.

Mr Petrov pauses and smiles, a secret, perhaps even a sentimental smile. 'If you cut me you will see it is salt water and not blood which runs through my veins.'

Professor Slotinowitz now interrupts. Well, I must say, *at least* he has the good manners to wait until there is a pause in Mr Petrov's story. 'Did you know,' he says in that know-all voice he uses, 'that the sturgeon fish is one of the oldest animals on our planet and has existed in much the same form for a hundred million years?' *Sheesh! He expects a busy person should know such rubbish?* Then he continues in the same school-teacher manner, 'Like the cockroach, which has existed for an equally long period with almost no further evolution, it is perfectly adapted for its function and environment.'

'Since when is a fish and an insect an *animal*, Professor? A fish is a fish and a cockroach is a lousy bug!' Mrs Z proclaims.

'Enough!' I say, never mind my lack of tact, which, believe me, is a commodity now certainly not called for. 'Who is telling this story anyway? Mrs Z? Or the professor? Or Mr Petrov here?' I turn to Mr P. 'Please continue, so far it is most interesting, although I, for one, have never tasted caviar.'

Mr Petrov smiles at me. 'Ah, Mrs Moses, then you have not eaten from the table of God himself! A big fish, a mighty sturgeon, grows up to four metres in length not counting the snout, which, by the way, it uses as a tool to scour the sea bed for food. The big fish are known as beluga and give the biggest grains of roe, and each grain is as black as a South Sea pearl. A single tiny grain, no bigger than the head of a match, when placed on the tongue and pressed lightly against the palate will *explode* in the mouth and the delicate and exotic taste will remain for an hour!'

Mr Petrov is warming up again and I hope

everyone now has the good manners not to continue interrupting. Though that is some fat hope with this lot of *meshuggeners*.

'The smaller fish are perhaps not so exotic but still precious and are of two sizes, the *ossetra* and then the smaller *sevruga*. The roe of these two smaller fish varies in colour from the light grey colour of the Tsar's battleships to an opaque tangerine. It is smaller in size and not so robust in flavour, but still a wonderful delicacy,' Mr Petrov explains and then pauses for just a moment. But a moment is all that's needed for Olga Zorbatov to wedge her way back into the conversation.

'My husband the chef,' she casts a baleful eye in the direction of the professor, 'who, I might remind a certain person who calls fishes and bugs animals, was *also* a professor, would bring half a kilo of the finest beluga home from the Grande Rex Hotel in a silver bowl filled with crushed ice. I'd chop a large onion nice and fine, mince two hard-boiled eggs and make several dozen tiny blini pancakes for our midnight rooftop supper. Then, watching the stars, we would dollop the beluga caviar onto the tiny pancakes as though it was cheap as duck's liver pâté, and then eat it all in one delicious ten-minute sitting!'

'A professor of star signs and chicken soup for the sick, if I remember correctly,' Professor Slotinowitz observes gratuitously to the moon.

There are several sniggers and I see that Mr Mendelsohn has covered his mouth with four slim fingers. I am quick to put a stop to any potential hilarity, as the last thing we want is a conniption from Olga Zorbatov. 'Now, now, enough already!' I admonish. 'You two must stop this bickering or Mr Petrov will not finish his story.

I glance over to Mr P to give him his cue to continue and see that the big, strong man, with hands that could throttle a bear, is crying. A bright tear runs slowly down both of his cheeks. He is by no means a handsome man, as too many flying sparks and iron pellets have burnt into the flesh of his face, which is now a permanent ruddy colour and rough as coarse sandpaper. But his tears give him the vulnerable look of a small boy who is very sad.

He looks over at Olga Z and slowly shakes his head. 'A thumbnail of beluga placed on one of your tiny pancakes is a sufficient and elegant beginning to a banquet. Caviar of such nobility, to be appreciated for its exquisite taste, should be treated with the greatest respect and used in the same manner as a miser hordes a pinch of golddust.' Mr Petrov slaps his big hand against his brow in a gesture of disbelief and then says in a slow measured tone, 'Mrs Z, to "dollop" such a brilliant creation is to shit in the mouth of God!'

Mr Petrov becomes aware of the presence of his spontaneous tears and quickly knuckles the wetness from his eyes. 'Excuse me, I am ashamed of myself,' he sniffs and tries to explain. 'You see, the tasting of caviar means a great deal to me. It is the reason I am here, the first of my village people to flee from Mother Russia in a thousand years.'

He looks up at the night sky and sniffs again and then he looks back at us, 'You must all be thinking: What does a blacksmith know of caviar? You would ordinarily be right, herring pie maybe, but not beluga caviar. No village fortunate enough to catch a big sturgeon fish would waste a single grain of its caviar on a humble fisherman, let alone allow a blacksmith near its precious beluga. Besides, it is not unfair to say, with his tongue singed from daily proximity to the foundry furnace, a blacksmith would have considerable trouble telling borscht from a plate of chicken soup.'

Mr Petrov stops to think for a moment and for

once there is complete silence from all of us, and only the sudden crackle of a twig on the fire is heard. Then he clears his throat:

The very best of beluga caviar carries with it the word 'malassol', which is a fancy term but means only that it is lightly salted. A woman may add a pinch of salt to a dish she is preparing, then stir and taste. If it is not salted enough she will add more until she is satisfied. If too salty she will add a little water. But with the best caviar it is different. The beluga can only be salted once, and if the salting is not correct the whole batch is spoiled. You see, the process by which the best Volga caviar is salted is an instinct and a great gift. The Salt is a prince among the river fishermen and his gift is so rare that the old women light a candle in every village church on every day of the year. And with it a prayer is offered to Saint Peter, the patron saint of fishermen, that the Salt lives to be a hundred years and that God's most precious gift, a 'beluga tongue', will be with him until the day he dies and goes straight to paradise, no stopping at the gate, no questions asked.

When I was twenty-five, the Salt, on whom all

the villages depended, died. He was very old, more than one hundred and seventeen years, and known the length and breadth of the great Volga River, which you may not know stretches 3,600 kilometres before it reaches the Caspian Sea. It was claimed that he was discovered to have the beluga tongue at the age of eighteen and for ninety-nine years it had never failed him, and not a single batch of beluga caviar was ever spoiled in the twenty villages strung along the eighty kilometres of river he worked. Village children like myself grew up thinking of him as only next to God and the Tsar in ranking and, because we had not met the other two gentlemen personally, perhaps more important.

At the news of his death all the village priests made a pilgrimage to the bishop's cathedral in the capital city while we all rushed into the village churches to pray that God would grant us the miracle of another beluga tongue. The bishop explained to the priests the method they should use to find another Salt.

The caviar buyers from Moscow, St Petersburg and Persia were invited to the convocation and informed that they must supply one hundred kilograms of the finest unsalted beluga caviar. This was in itself a king's ransom and the dealers argued and pleaded with the holy bishop to make it one hundred lots of one hundred grams instead. But the bishop held his ground and showed the greedy middlemen that the correct amount was stipulated in the five-hundred-year-old tome, The Book of River Rights, which was the final authority on how the Salt must be chosen. Finally, after much wringing of hands and crying poor, they agreed to make the supply of unsalted beluga caviar available.

The ancient method of finding a beluga tongue was quite simple. A hundred unmarried men must be picked at random and each given a kilogram of the finest beluga caviar. From this fortune in fish eggs each man must pick a single tiny egg and place it, as the Salt has always done, on his tongue. Then he has to roll it around his palate and when it 'explodes' determine the exact amount of salt needed in the finest Volga beluga set out in front of him. If he gets it wrong he will have spoiled a fortune in the best beluga caviar, and will forever be known in his village as a 'rotten egg' and, no matter how great his skill, he will never again be included in a fishing boat that hunts the sturgeon. Of course, if he gets it right, and is discovered to have a beluga tongue, his fortune is made and he will be a rich and honoured man until the day he dies and this hopefully at a very ripe old age.

'Excuse me, Mr Petrov.' It is Anya Mendelsohn (she is not married to her violinist, but what's in a name?) who speaks quietly, then waits for further permission. We are all very much surprised, as she has never interrupted a story before. Anya holds her baby to her breast as Mr P nods in her direction. 'Excuse me, please,' she repeats, 'but what does a man know of salting a fish dish? Surely this is women's work!' She waves a dismissive hand. 'A fish egg is a fish egg, roe is roe, salt is salt, taste is taste, so tell me, please already, what's so special about this beluga fish egg that a good female cook cannot judge its salt?'

Anya's question makes sense and all the women look towards Mr Petrov, who has now suddenly turned an even more furious crimson colour and his whole body has begun to shake. 'It . . . it . . . c-c-cannot be done by a woman,' he stammers.

'And why not?' Mrs Z demands imperiously, one eye half closed, the opposite eyebrow arched.

'I . . . I . . . c-c-cannot explain,' Mr Petrov

stammers again and it is obvious that he is mortified by Anya's question.

'But why not?' Anya asks in a most reasonable voice. 'A woman is trained from childhood in these things, her palate is accustomed to tasting for salt and herbs and the absence or presence of the right quantity of all sorts of subtle flavours and secret ingredients.'

'Yes, like mushrooms!' Mrs Z says, ever the tactful one.

Mr Petrov is now even more visibly disturbed and bites his lower lip so that I think at any moment it will start to bleed. The perspiration is running down his brow and his hands shake even more than before. 'Her blood, her m-m-m-monthly blood,' he blurts out at last. 'It . . . is . . . her blood which will spoil the caviar for the whole season!'

There is a collective gasp and it is now our turn for embarrassment. We have forced poor Mr Petrov into an impossible confession.

'As a Jew I can understand this,' I say hurriedly. 'In our law a woman is considered unclean when it comes that time of the month for her. She is forbidden to prepare food for her husband and must take a bath in the *mikvah* at the completion of her cycle.

Your Volga River fishermen would make good Jews and also, believe you me, a nice plate of *gefilte* fish would be most welcome.'

I look around and can see that everyone is grateful for this explanation and Mrs Moses, who is of course me, is granted top marks for tact and diplomacy! Then I say, 'Please continue, Mr Petrov, tell us how you look for this person who will have a beluga tongue, which we now understand can't be a female for what you already explained are very good and sound reasons.' I smile and in a cheerful voice say, 'If this caviar is as nice as you say, there must be a great many volunteers among the young men, I think, not so?'

I say all this except for the last sentence in rapid fire so it will come out too quickly for any of us to think too much about the big embarrassment we have caused. But still quickly enough to get us back on track and to act like Anya's question didn't happen, not at all and, if it did, is already forgotten and not ever to be mentioned again, if you know what I mean?

Mr Petrov is by no means a stupid man and he gives me a grateful look. 'No, no, no volunteers, Mrs Moses! The selection of one hundred men must be hand-picked by God. The priest in every village, all twenty, must choose five unmarried men by a very special method. In each village the Holy Father will select a tree or a rock or a point on the riverbank, or any object his prayers have pointed out to him in a vision. He will then go to that object and sprinkle it with holy water and anoint it with precious oils. This must be done at the dead of night when the village is asleep. Then the first five unmarried men in every village to pass this tree or rock or fishing boat or holy point which has been decided upon by God through his holy servant will be those chosen to salt the beluga.

'But what if all should fail?' Mr Mendelsohn the violinist asks.

'Ah, that is the miracle! It has never been known to fail, there is always a new beluga tongue who comes to light. Saint Peter the Fisherman has never deserted us.' Mr Petrov stops and absently scratches the tip of his nose with his forefinger. 'Except once, when the holy saint of all the world's fishermen picked the village blacksmith to be the new beluga tongue.'

'You!' we all chorus. 'You were the one chosen!'

Mr Petrov nods sadly, then continues his story.

· · ·

In our village the priest chose to sprinkle the holy water on the anvil and then to anoint it with oil. The blacksmith's shop is on the edge of the village and is almost on the banks of the river, and the fishermen, who rise at dawn to go to their boats, are forced to pass it. Besides, the anvil, which is used for the shoeing of horses and mules, stands outside the blacksmith's shop in a most convenient position, close to the path leading down to where the boats are. So, by accident, because I too rise early to fire the furnace, I was included in the first five men to pass the anvil and was picked with four young fishermen friends to represent our village.

On a prescribed day we travelled to the bishop's cathedral in the capital fifty kilometres away. When we arrived we were each given a small wooden disc with a loop of leather strung through it and told to hang it around our neck. On each disc was a number, which also appeared painted carefully on the side of a pure white porcelain bowl that, after being washed in holy water, was handed to us wrapped in new muslin cloth. We entered the cathedral and were made to sit cross-legged in rows on the marble floor and were then shown how to spread the muslin cloth in front of us and place the numbered bowl exactly at its centre. Beside it a priest placed a small bowl of white Siberian salt, and a pair of tiny pinewood tweezers wrapped in new cheesecloth so that they could not be contaminated before being used. The bishop gave thanks to God and to Saint Peter the Fisherman and said Holy Mass, and each of the candidates received the wine and the host from the bishop's own hand. Then all were required to drink from a silver chalice of water to rinse out their mouths before spitting the water into a basin held by a novitiate. After this ritual was completed, the cathedral doors were locked, and into each bowl was measured exactly one kilo of precious beluga caviar.

This kilogram of finest unsalted beluga was more valuable on the markets of the European cities than all the money each of us might earn in a lifetime. In just a few minutes all but one kilogram would be spoiled forever, ninety-nine kilograms of the food God created to be eaten in heaven would be destroyed by the addition of too much or too little salt. We waited for a final blessing from the bishop and then the salting of the beluga began.

Mr Petrov stopped and looked around at us, as the food in The Family Frying Pan was almost cooked, and even though we were all hungry I could see that there were none among us who did not wish him to continue.

I have mentioned the procedure before but I will repeat it in just the way it happened to me. With the wooden tweezers I selected a single fish egg, a single precious grain, a tiny pearl of glory, and placed it carefully on the tip of my tongue. I had never before tasted this priceless jewel of the sea and now I rolled it around my palate as if I was imbued with an ancient instinct. The tiny ball of ecstasy seemed to dance on my tongue and skate across my palate as though it knew exactly where to go to stimulate my tastebuds. Quite suddenly there was an explosion in my head as loud, I swear, as a single cannon shot fired beside my ear. With it came a burst of the most exotic and exquisite flavour I had ever experienced. My eyes rolled back with divine pleasure and I began to moan. My arm lifted of its own accord and to my surprise I saw that I now held the tiny wooden spoon. Then my hand moved, again without any conscious effort on my part, and dipped the wooden spoon into the bowl of salt and sprinkled it over the beluga caviar in the bowl. Without hesitation and as if by magic, it returned and dipped once more into the salt and added yet another spoonful, then again, though this time slightly less. Still inwardly directed, I mixed the salt into the beluga, but with so little hand movement that my fingers hardly seemed to move.

All of this occurred without a single thought entering my head and, when the mixing was complete, again without any rational decision from me, my hand collapsed into my lap and lost all its power. In fact, if I had wished to raise it to add more salt to the beluga I would not have been able to do so. But what lingered was the sublime taste, the unforgettable aftertaste of the single sturgeon's egg in my mouth.

I have no idea how long I sat waiting for the cathedral bells to ring, for I seemed to be in some sort of trance. But at last they rang out and the enormous doors were flung open. We rose and, leaving the salted caviar in the bowls behind, were ushered out into the great square to wait. It was now the dealers' turn to enter the great church.

There were twelve of these rich caviar merchants in their long woollen coats and shiny boots who are known as the Twelve Apostles of Beluga and they were responsible for 'The Tasting of the Salt'. Five were chosen from Moscow, five from St Petersburg and two from Persia. Each had been selected for his immense knowledge of the sturgeon's roe and the exceptional clarity of his taste for the finest beluga caviar. Each carried with him a pair of tiny tweezers made of pure gold with which he must now select a single egg from each of the hundred bowls and, having tasted it, mark it for its perfection of salt. No word was spoken between them, and they would simply write down the number of the bowl they had selected and hand it to the bishop.

You may imagine my surprise when a priest came hurrying from the cathedral calling out a number, my number! The decision by the Twelve Apostles of Beluga had been unanimous and soon, with the church filled and with onlookers spilling over into the square and the bells ringing, the bishop announced my number again from the high altar.

Everyone claimed it was a miracle. A blacksmith and not a fisherman had been given the beluga tongue by Peter the saint of all fishermen. In all of history such a thing had never happened before. Some of the old *babushka* immediately forecast that no good would come of it. But, of course, they were ignored, as most old women are in these modern times. 'The holy saint of fishermen,' the bishop explained, 'worked in his own mysterious ways', and the fact that the gift of a beluga tongue was given to a blacksmith made it no lesser than a great miracle. I was proclaimed the Salt of the twenty villages with a grand ceremony and a procession that led through the city streets, which was followed by a banquet held by the caviar merchants and attended by the city's most important dignitaries. It was an occasion so auspicious that a person of my humble origin could not comprehend that men could aspire to such extravagant feasting. The food was far too rich for my blacksmith's palate and the vodka was of such purity that it must have been distilled from the tears of God.

In my own village we feasted for days on herring pie, roast lamb and sweetmeats of every kind. I was a hero who had put our village on the map and bestowed great honour on all our fisherfolk. Henceforth, no beluga fish would leave our stretch of the Volga without first having been salted by me.

Needless to say, I was forced to give up blacksmithing, for I was by definition a rich man who owned a horse and trap, and wore shiny boots and a coat that touched the ground. The candles in the village churches were lit for me with prayers for my good health, and children stepped aside and cheered as I passed. There seemed no end to my good fortune, except for one thing, the Salt must by holy tradition remain celibate, and I was forbidden to know the joy of a woman in my bed.

I told myself that if a priest can take a vow of chastity and keep to it all of his life, then I too can overcome the primitive urge which conquers the minds of the strongest men. I was strong-willed by nature and single-minded in my endeavour to live up to my vocation and commitment to my people. To strengthen this resolve I reminded myself that I had been granted the gift of a beluga tongue from Saint Peter the Fisherman himself. It would be a small price to pay and I counted myself fortunate that with five spinster sisters to attend to my needs I possessed all the blessings of a married man save for connubial bliss.

As to the job at hand, it seemed I was truly gifted. On every occasion I was called upon to travel to a village where they had made a killing of the sturgeon, it was the same result. I made no conscious decisions myself but no sooner had the precious jewel, the tiny black marble of pristine perfection, exploded on my tongue when my hand, moved by the Holy Spirit and guided by the Great Fisherman himself, moved to the salt pot of its own accord. Consequently the salting of the beluga was always performed to perfection, and the term *malassol* on a blue can of Volga caviar from our region of the river became especially prized by the caviar merchants.

My reputation grew to the point where, in a few short years, my name became a legend right up into the furthermost reaches of the Volga. Soon all the big, important fish, the most precious and glorious beluga, carefully packed in ice, were brought from far beyond our river boundaries for me to sanctify with 'the gift of salt'.

And then one day as I was travelling in my trap to a village not ten kilometres away, where they had taken two great beluga fish that very morning, I saw a young woman limping at the side of the road. Her hair was the colour of flax and braided around her head in so many strands that I felt sure that if it was allowed to fall, it would surely have reached well below her slender waist. She looked up at me as I passed and her eyes were the colour of the summer sky, though they were filled with pain and distress and I could see that she was close to tears.

I quickly brought my trap to a halt and, climbing down, walked the short distance to where she stood. She bowed her head and modestly averted her eyes and as I addressed her I felt sure that she knew who I was but she felt herself too humble to look at me.

'Good morning, little sister, are you hurt?' I asked gently. 'Where are you going?'

Without replying to my first question, she gave the name of the village to which I myself was travelling.

'Come, you may ride with me, my name is Petrov Petrovitch and, while I am a big fellow, there is room on the trap for both of us.'

'I cannot, sir,' she said, without looking up. 'I am not a married woman.'

'But you are hurt, people will understand.'

'My father will beat me, it would not be correct.' She looked up for the first time and smiled, and it was as though an arrow had been shot through my heart. I know this mention of cupid's arrow is not an original idea, but there is no other way to describe the sensation. One moment my heart was beating in my chest as calmly as the ticking of the gold watch attached to the chain strung across my stomach and the next it was as though . . . well, as though it had been penetrated by an arrow!

I swallowed hard, attempting to stay composed. 'Do you know who I am?' I asked.

'Yes, sir, you are the Salt,' she said quietly, her eyes once again downcast.

'Well then, your father will know you are safe with me. Come along, I will help you up into my trap.' I took her arm by the elbow and she limped to the trap. I could now see that she was in considerable pain. I grabbed her by her slim waist and lifted her into the seat. My big hands seemed to enclose her entire form, and I could feel the warm flesh under her coarse linen skirt. I am ashamed to say my throat tightened and went suddenly dry, and I was forced to cough in an attempt to conceal my extreme agitation. As she was now on the trap seat and her ankle was at the level of my waist, I could see that it was red and inflamed.

'You have sprained it badly, perhaps even broken it,' I said clumsily, my voice sounding strange to me as though it had risen another octave.

'No, sir, it was a scorpion.'

'A scorpion!' I exclaimed, my dismay immediately apparent. It would take us half an hour of hard driving to reach her village. I anxiously looked again at the ankle and saw that the colour of her foot and the surrounding area was rapidly turning a deep scarlet and was beginning to spread up her leg as the poison travelled up to her heart. The sting from a large scorpion can kill, and I saw the two tiny marks where the creature had struck her on the arch of her instep, injecting its deadly poison directly into the vein that lies near the surface of the skin. It is a large vein, I have since learned, called the Long Saphenous, and rides from the instep up the entire length of the leg, and is an easy passage for the blood pumping its way back to the heart.

I looked at the stricken girl and could see that she was in terrible pain. I knew instantly that we could not make the distance to the village in time to save her life. All fishermen carry a sharp gutting knife on their belts and, although I was now perceived to be a gentleman and had never been a fisherman, it was a habit carried over from childhood when I had worked on the boats.

I reached for the knife and at the same time

spoke to the girl. 'I am going to cut the bite and try to suck the poison out.' I grabbed the trap whip which had a handle of plaited leather and handed it to her. 'Here, bite hard onto this!' She nodded, but by now the pain was so intense that she moaned and sobbed, and her hands shook violently as she took the small leather whip and bit down hard.

Using the gutting knife I cut deep into the scorpion puncture marks, opening the flesh on the instep where the vein is still fairly small, and even closer to the surface. Putting my mouth against the wound, I sucked and immediately spat. I continued for several minutes tasting her fresh blood in my mouth and spitting it onto the ground at my feet. I hoped I had acted swiftly enough to suck most of the poison from the vein, sufficient anyway, to prevent it from killing her.

At one stage I glanced up at the girl and saw that she had the handle of the trap whip grimly clamped between her teeth and that her eyes were tightly closed against the pain and her cheeks were wet with tears of distress. My heart went out to this beautiful young woman who was suffering so much. I continued to suck and spit for another five minutes and then I took a small flask of vodka from the pocket of my coat and poured a little of it on the open wound. I held my thumb hard against the vein to stop the blood flow. After I had rinsed my mouth with a swig of vodka and spat the contents out, I removed the trap whip from the girl's mouth. 'Here, drink!' I said, holding the flask to her lips. Even in this state of severe distress her lips looked soft and inviting, and I am ashamed to say I felt the stirring deep inside me again and the pain in my heart returned. She parted her lips to take the vodka and coughed as the fiery liquid reached her throat, but she managed to keep it down.

I removed my coat and placed it over her shoulders and wrapped it around her to keep her warm. Then I tore the sleeve from my blouse and made a tourniquet above her knee, blushing violently as I raised her skirt to tie and then to tighten the bandage. Quite soon the blood flow began to lessen and, wrenching the remaining sleeve from my arm, I bandaged her foot. Then I leapt up into the trap and we set off at a furious pace for the village.

You can see I am not a small man and the seat of the trap was not very wide and so her body, enveloped in my coat, was forced against mine. Although the coat was of fine heavy wool and I now tell myself I couldn't possibly have felt her ravishing body through the thick material, it was as though she wore nothing. The flesh of her thigh was pressed against my own and, despite her condition, I thought I must surely die of the pure ecstasy. I could do nothing to stop the feelings that coursed through my blood and the terrible beating of my sinful heart, and I prayed silently to Saint Peter the Fisherman to make my thoughts pure and stop the ache in my throat.

Twice on the way she vomited, but the tourniquet effectively cut the blood supply from her leg so that by the time we reached the village it was clear that I had been successful in sucking out most of the scorpion's poison and that she would live.

I was late for the caviar salting. I carried her into her father's cottage and instructed her mother to remove the tourniquet above her knee. Her young brother had been sent to fetch an old crone, who was said to know how to treat a scorpion bite. I departed, but not before learning her name was Katya Markova.

'It is a love story! A beautiful love story!' Tamara Polyansky cries, clapping her hands together in excitement. 'Mr Petrov, you had fallen in love and . . .' She stops in mid-sentence, as no doubt Miss Showbiz with the slow-motion brain suddenly remembers that women are forbidden to someone who possesses a beluga tongue. Tamara now brings her hands to her mouth, which has formed into an 'o' of consternation.

'Oh dear, I am so sorry, I am so very sorry, Mr Petrov,' she says in a small, pathetic voice.

Mr Petrov sighs, then smiles a sad smile and spreads his hands. 'You are quite right, Miss Polyansky, I was hopelessly in love. Head over heels in love, besotted and enchanted and unable to think of anything else but the beautiful Katya Markova.'

In a week the news had spread around the villages and the village priest came to see me. 'Is it true, Petrov Petrovitch?' he asked.

'Holy Father, I am pure in my heart,' I told him. 'I have not taken Katya Markova into my bed, but I cannot deny she has entered my heart.'

'You cannot have her, Petrov Petrovitch, you are the Salt. Would you destroy the livelihood of twenty villages for a silly girl?'

'Father, I have prayed to God and to Saint Peter the Fisherman all night for four nights that my heart will be mended, that the love I feel for Katya Markova will be taken from me, wrung from my heart like a sea sponge. I simply don't know how I shall endure the pain of it if it continues for I am aware that I cannot have her and I will live with this, and pray that God will forgive the thoughts in my head and the desire in my heart. I shall swear on the Holy Bible that I will not take Katya Markova to my bed, and will remain the Salt for as long as I am needed by the river people.'

'Bless you, my son! You will one day enter the gates of paradise to the clapping of angels' wings and the sounding of trumpets!' Then he added, 'A woman is a wonderful thing for a man, but a beluga tongue, now that is something else!'

Mr Petrov looks up and shrugs and it seems he had come to the end of his story which, I must say, I didn't consider a very good ending. The boyski doesn't get the girlski and all that's left is a fish mouth? Life goes on ho hum, so to speak. What kind of garbage is that? A miserable ending, no less!

'So tell me already, Mr P,' I say in a sweet voice which hides my disappointment. 'You remained the Salt and you were rich and famous and daily

candles were lit and prayers said on your behalf.
And you drove a horse and trap and wore shiny
boots up to your knees and a pure wool coat that
swept the ground, so how come you're sitting on
that log with patches on your *toukis*?'

The others all laugh, but in a good-natured way.
Mr Petrov has three patches on the back of his
trousers and each is of a different colour, one red,
the other blue and the last brown. He is a practical
man, but for neatness and sewing he knows from
nothing already.

'That is a very good question, Mrs Moses.' Mr
Petrov looks at The Family Frying Pan bubbling on
the fire and then at all of us, knowing that we are all
hungry and that the food is ready. 'That is, if you
are still interested?'

'Ye . . . es . . . er,' everyone says, but in a tone
which contains a certain degree of politeness, and I
can see that the demands of an empty stomach are
greater than the need for another empty ending.

'A good ending should not be served to an
empty stomach,' I say. 'First we eat and then the
ending will be even more satisfying.' Such a diplomat I am becoming already, I think to myself.

After we have eaten, turnips and cabbage mixed

with a little fat and with three large potatoes, not so bad, Mr Petrov concludes his story.

'With the story of my love affair with Katya Markova put to rest by the priests in every village church, who, no doubt instructed by the bishop, all preach a sermon about the triumph of the spirit over the needs of the flesh, honour and dignity is restored. Candles burn again at the altar of Saint Peter the Fisherman, giving thanks to the saint for having saved the situation. The general conclusion among the fishermen is that a beluga tongue is a great blessing and, besides, is a gift from God and the saint himself, whereas a woman is only gossip and trouble and, in the end, no gift at all.'

'Ha!' Olga Zorbatov snorts.

'But what of Katya? Does she love you? Is her heart broken?' Tamara Polyansky, Miss Showbiz, asks.

'It is a complete mystery to me that Katya should love a great clumsy person like me,' Mr Petrov says. 'But from the first moment she sees me after she has recovered from the scorpion sting it becomes obvious to all that she only has eyes for me. That our love is a precious thing that has been made in heaven.'

'Yuk!' I think to myself, this is getting past even sloppy.

'You made the right decision, the economic welfare of twenty villages was more important,' the professor announced. 'No question about it.'

'More important than love?' Anya, who has never been heard to raise her voice, asks, incredulous. 'Nothing in the world is more important than love, Professor!' Then she adds in a soft and disappointed voice, 'You made the *wrong* decision, Petrov Petrovitch.'

'There is more,' Mr Petrov said.

Two weeks after the scorpion incident, news came from Moscow that the consignment of beluga I had salted directly after leaving Katya at her father's cottage had arrived spoiled. Three days later from St Petersburg came another angry message. The caviar from twenty great beluga fish, the biggest catch of the season and worth millions of roubles, and all salted by me, had also arrived spoiled. And then more and more, every beluga fish I had touched from the day of the scorpion was found on its arrival to be unfit for consumption.

There was only one answer possible and it was

contained within the heads and spilled from the lips of every villager. I had told a lie and had secretly taken Katya Markova into my bed.

The rumour soon spread that I had been seen in a cornfield with her and that I had been making love to her when the scorpion stung her on the instep. I had broken my vow and lied to a holy priest and therefore to Saint Peter the Fisherman and to God Himself! I had destroyed them all and must be destroyed myself and all that I possessed should be given as a penance to the Church.

It was the rough justice of the fisherfolk and would be more merciful than the torture and humiliation the caviar merchants would demand. I would simply be taken out on the great river and dropped over the side of the boat too far to swim back to shore.

I was forbidden to see my beloved Katya, but allowed a visit from my five sisters. I forgot to tell you that my parents had passed away several years before. This caused a great deal of crying and distress, but I knew, at least, that they would be well taken care of, even though they would forever remain spinsters. I had publicly disgraced my family and there could be no forgiveness, not even the poorest peasant would now take such soiled goods as his bride. Before the priest came to confiscate all my possessions I had buried gold coins in a secret place which they had been told about.

As they took their leave, Anna, the oldest of my sisters, kissed me and whispered, 'God be with you, Petrov Petrovitch, and have mercy on your soul. We have decided to use the money you have given us to emigrate to New York and we will take Katya Markova with us so she will be safe.'

I was taken out at dawn, when the grey mist hung over the great river. Twelve of the village elders, all fishermen except for the priest, accompanied me in the fishing boat. After two hours, when we had reached the centre of the widest stretch of the Volga, where it was impossible for any man to swim back to the shore, the donkey engine was cut. The men sang the great song of our river and the priest heard my confession. When I did not confess that I had made love to my beloved Katya Markova, he demanded that I do so.

'You will not be granted absolution, my son. You will forever burn in hell! You must confess at once!'

'Holy Father, I cannot confess to what I have not done!' I cried.

'Lies!' one of the fishermen shouted. 'How else

could the caviar spoil? Not once, but twenty times!' There was a chorus of approval at this remark. But I would not confess. I knew that Saint Peter the Fisherman would know I was telling the truth and he is a greater authority before God than a village priest.

Mr Petrov looks up and shrugs. 'So they threw me overboard and started the donkey engine and in a moment the boat was lost in the mist. I knew that soon I must drown, that the strength in my arms would eventually forsake me and that I would sink under the gloomy black water.'

'But you didn't! Here you are with us!' Mr Mendelsohn cries, obviously delighted at this happy outcome.

Mr Petrov grins. 'God is good. I struck out for the shore, thinking that I should die exhausted rather than simply give in to my fate and sink to the bottom of the river. I had almost reached the end of my strength when I bumped into something floating in the mist. It was a large heavy object, which I grabbed, though it was not easy to hold onto. It was a beluga fish, a dead sturgeon of massive size floating on the surface. I was fortunate for it was late summer and the water was not yet cold. Two days later we reached the estuary to the Caspian Sea, a distant shore well beyond the twenty villages and, like Jonah himself, I was saved by a great fish.'

'It was her blood!' Tamara Polyansky says suddenly. 'The blood you sucked from the scorpion sting! It was a woman's blood and it caused the spoiling of the caviar!'

Mr Petrov shakes his head and laughs. 'No, not so, my dear Tamara Polyansky, I think maybe there is too much showbiz in *your* blood. As I floated downstream holding onto the dead fish I saw many others also dead in the river. There was a mysterious disease among the sturgeon that year and this is now a well-established fact. The roe, the precious beluga, carries the disease, and though it could not yet be tasted in a single grain of caviar, it was already potentially spoiled long before I salted it.'

We all applaud this splendid ending. 'And now we know your destination when we get out of Russia,' I declare happily.

'Yes, Mrs Moses, that is quite true,' Mr Petrov replies. 'I shall go to New York to find my beloved Katya Markova.'

MISS SHOWBIZ
AND THE
DEATH OF COUNT TOLSTOY

Miss Showbiz, Tamara Polyansky, came to me this morning. 'I'm ready, Mrs Moses,' she said.

'About time if I may say so.' I say this not without a little bite of sarcasm. 'The others have been gone nearly an hour looking for tonight's dinner and here is Miss Showbiz, Tamara Polyansky, still hanging around.

'No, not ready for that!' she exclaims. She has her hand around the top of a sack and now releases it, and bends and grabs the bottom corners and upends it. Out roll potatoes and beets, half a sack full and not one bad or mouldy. 'There! Satisfied?' she says smugly.

I am astonished at such a rich haul, but I can't let her see this. 'Don't be impertinent, Tamara Polyansky. You know our rules.'

It's funny me talking to Tamara like this, I am the youngest of us all, not yet twenty, and Tamara is twenty-six and very pretty with green eyes and blonde hair, a real Russian that one. She's worked in the circus, knows her way around men and is a bit of a flirt, even with someone as flirt-proof as the professor. Her body is as supple as a snake's and she spends most of her free time doing complicated gymnastics. The children say she can do a double backflip, then a somersault and land back on her feet just like that. But personally I have not seen this and, if I did, I would wonder what a lady was doing throwing her legs around and being definitely indecent in terms of what she shows in the process.

'I'm sorry, Mrs Moses,' she now says. 'I was doing my exercises and forgot the time.'

I point accusingly to the vegetables at my feet. 'You haven't been out this morning, so where did these come from?'

Tamara Polyansky shrugs her pretty shoulders. 'I don't know, the sack was there at my feet when I woke this morning.'

Unlike most of us, Tamara still cares about her looks, and her hair is neatly braided, her face scrubbed and her lips stained carefully with blackberry juice. Even her patched dress and coat somehow look more stylish on her thin body than Mrs Solomon's still excellent coat looks on me. She is not a Mrs but a Miss and, unlike myself, doesn't pretend otherwise.

I sigh and give her a hard look. 'Tamara, God is good, and with His help we will maybe someday get out of Russia, but so far He hasn't started to leave food in a sack at our feet when we wake up?'

Tamara Polyansky's eyes grow wide, 'You don't think I . . . ?' she cries.

'Tamara, men are your absolute known weakness. Who gave you this food?'

It is hard being a leader. It would be so nice sometimes just to follow for a while. You know, just put one foot in front of the other with somebody else doing the thinking and taking the responsibility for our safety, patching up the quarrels between people and worrying about what we will find to eat every long, tiring day on the road.

Sometimes, when I feel the stretch and the itch of the large, horrible crescent-shaped purple scar where the frying pan burned through my flesh as we were running away from the Tsar's marauding troopers, I wish that the so-called miracle of the invincible Mrs Moses had never occurred. But then, on the other hand, I think, I'd be dead from the first soldier's sword thrust into my back. So never mind a little scar, compared to being dead, I must say here and now being the leader of this bunch of no-hopers is definitely better.

Now I look steadily at Tamara Polyansky and my eyes narrow. She might be Miss Showbiz, but I know a little myself from acting. 'It was the boy from the village, wasn't it? That young man who followed us all yesterday afternoon? Followed you! You could practically see his tongue hanging out and not only his tongue!'

Tamara lowers her eyes and nods her head. 'I swear I only gave him a little kiss, a tiny peck on the cheek.'

'Tamara? Look at me. Say that and look me straight in the eye.'

'No! I swear it! On my mother's grave!' Now she looks up at me, appealing for mercy. 'You won't throw me out, please, Mrs Moses?'

'A kiss? Then another kiss and then another and

what follows after these kisses is another kind of acrobatics you also learned in the circus, eh?' I say accusingly. 'You have put us all in terrible danger, Tamara Polyansky!'

Tamara's eyes brim with tears. 'Believe me, please, I beg you!' She begins to sob. 'He, he, looked just like my Eugene, the spitting image.' She looks up tearfully, 'I couldn't help myself, it was just a little kiss. Like kissing a beautiful ghost!'

I am not so stupid that I ask who is this Eugene. To know is to allow her to change the subject. Maybe later I'll get the juicy bits. 'We are in danger!' I shout. 'Terrible danger! We have to leave now! At once! Go and find the others, tell them there is already food for tonight, never mind the mushrooms, we have to leave immediately.'

I am angry, but at the same time I wonder what a kiss feels like. In my village the first kiss you get from a man is on your wedding night. Kissing is strictly off limits at all other times and occasions. Maybe that's why I am so angry with Tamara and her ghost kisser. Here she is kissing and smooching like it's going out of style, and I'm stuck with leading a bunch of misfits out of the wilderness. I call myself Mrs and I've never even been kissed.

'I'm sorry, Mrs Moses, I didn't mean no harm. I swear it was only a kiss, nothing more.'

Yes, young lady, for you only a kiss, I think to myself, for me it would be an earthquake. But on the outside I stay calm.

'Tamara Polyansky!' I point out. 'Maybe it was just a kiss. As a matter of fact I believe you. But this young man goes back to his village and boasts of your kiss. You know how it is. He tells all his friends and hints it was, well, you know, *more* than a kiss, a *lot* more than a kiss and he rolls his eyes and gets a dreamy look on his stupid peasant face. They drink a little vodka and next thing they all arrive, all the young men from the village with one thing on their minds, and it isn't a sack of potatoes and beets!'

'I didn't think, Mrs Moses.' She stamps her foot. 'I am so stupid! It will not happen again. Please! If you make me leave I will surely die!'

'For God's sake, woman!' I yell at her, mostly so she can't see I'm jealous, but I am also worried, I have seen what a group of drunken peasants can do. 'Go and fetch the others, we have to get moving!'

Tamara grabs me and gives me a quick hug, 'Thank you, Mrs Moses, thank you from the bottom of my heart.' She leaves, running in the direction of a small forest of oak trees where Olga Zorbatov has been told by her husband in the sky that there will be blackberries and mushrooms. Anya, the mushroom expert, is leading this morning's expedition.

You can kiss goodbye the mushrooms and blackberries, mushrooms with potatoes and maybe a little borscht and then fresh blackberries, that would be very nice. But now, suddenly, with the recall of the Olga Zorbatov Psychic Expedition, it's potatoes and beet. Not so bad really, I console myself, at least our stomachs will be full tonight.

We will have to retrace our steps, I think to myself. We will go back around the village we passed through yesterday in a wide circle, so that if we are followed by a gang of sex-crazed youths they will think we have moved on further down the road. It means two days lost, maybe three. I must try to get us out of Russia before winter comes. I don't think the professor with his pains could survive another Russian winter and Anya Mendelsohn's baby, born last spring, could be another casualty.

. . .

It is late afternoon and we've been back on the road several hours, going of course in the wrong direction, when I suddenly remember what Tamara Polyansky said to me in the first place before the debacle of the ghost kiss. 'I'm ready, Mrs Moses.'

I approach her as we make camp in a small copse of trees where we can't be seen from the road. She has avoided me all day and even helped Anya with the baby. 'Ready for what?' I ask.

'Huh?' she says defensively, thinking perhaps that I am back on the attack.

I smile to reassure her. 'Tamara, what happened this morning is all over between us, completely forgotten and only to be remembered if you do it again! When you came up to me this morning you said you were ready. Ready for what?'

'Why, to tell my story, Mrs Moses. I thought with all the nice food we'd have tonight, you know what's in the sack and all, if I didn't tell it as well as the others it wouldn't matter so much. I mean all of our stomachs would be full from the potatoes and beet and people would have more patience, you know if . . .' She shrugs as if to explain, 'Well, I'm a trapeze artist, not a storyteller.'

I laugh. 'Tonight then, Tamara.' I give her a hug.

'I'm sure it will be very good.' A leader has to encourage also sometimes.

Everyone is tired and a bit grumpy, because today was supposed to have been a rest day. The morning was to be spent scrounging for food and the afternoon for bathing ourselves in the river and washing our clothes, doing some shoe repairs, sewing patches to worn garments and general maintenance. A haircut, a corn or blister treated or a pedicure given by one of the latest recruits to our little group, Mitya Shebaldin, a widow of sixty who seems to know a lot about feet but who can say why, she admits only to having once been a doctor's wife. No questions asked, a foot doctor we need.

Though we are going backwards the promise of a good meal has cheered us all up a bit. Anya found the mushrooms before Tamara arrived. How does Olga Zorbatov do that? No blackberries though. Tonight, in the food department anyway, we are all happy.

Tamara is wearing her good blue dress, which has no patches, and she's let her hair down and combed it until it shines in the firelight like spun gold. She has large green eyes that are very beautiful, and I think to myself that there is no point being jealous when someone is so far ahead in the beauty business.

I have dark hair with a funny blob of a nose and my mouth is too big, though I think maybe that I have nice eyes, dark but nice. But Tamara is tall with a beautiful bosom. As a matter of fact, when Mr Petrov was talking about his lost – hopefully one day to be found again in New York – Katya Markova, who remember is also a blonde with green eyes, I thought she must be a bit like Tamara. But when Tamara tries to flirt with Mr Petrov, who is a big man and still full of vigour, she is no more successful than with the professor, so maybe not. When you are a brunette all blondes look the same. Titch! There I go starting to be jealous again.

Tonight we have eaten first, because Tamara has requested this for the reasons already given. Also, she has confided in me that her story involves a cake, a large pink cake, and, as she rightly points out, cake comes *after* fish with potatoes and mushrooms. I almost forgot to mention the fish. Mr Petrov caught a large eel in the fishtrap he'd made and left in the river overnight, so that last night, when the ghost kisser came to visit Tamara and left his sack, it became more than just a potato and beet night. It was an eel night too and also when Olga Z's husband went hunting for mushrooms in the cosmos, a mushroom night. Some night, eh? So tonight, thanks to all these goings on, we have just completed a feast to remember. We can only hope, with our stomachs full for the first time in weeks, that the story of the pink cake doesn't send us all to sleep before we can taste a single imaginary slice.

Now, Tamara begins her tale:

I was an only child and my father doted on me. He was a fur trader and he dealt almost exclusively in mink, sable and ermine which he exported to Germany, America, France and Britain. He always said the Germans bought ermine because they were vulgar, the Americans mink because their money was new and they didn't know any better, while the French and the English, both much admired by my dear papa, bought sable because it was neither vulgar nor ostentatious, and cost considerably more than the other two furs.

As you may gather we were wealthy and lived in a big house with a great many servants and I was taught to do all the things rich little girls must do if they are to marry into the right kind of family.

Which, in my mother's eyes, meant the next step up the social scale into the minor nobility. I took private music, singing and dancing classes. The dancing master, Eugene Wilenski, was still a student at the Académie de Danse. I learned about French cuisine and practised English table manners, and by the time I was twelve I could accompany my parents almost anywhere without causing them embarrassment.

Oh, yes, I almost forgot the most important part. To amuse a young child with too much energy, who didn't much care for the stilted movements of the waltz and the polite restraints of the polka, my dancing master taught me a little of acrobatics. A few backflips and standing somersaults and how to balance and walk on my hands. I think I would have liked to have learned ballet but my mother had strictly forbidden this for reasons of her own which she never explained to me.

Eugene Wilenski came from a poor family and his brothers and sisters as well as his parents were acrobats and he too had been trained to the trapeze and gymnastics but was now a scholarship student at the academy and thought to be a promising dancer. I knew almost at once that my mind and my body could not be separated, and that the exhilaration of twisting and flipping in the air as though I were flying was the most wonderful experience I could possibly imagine. Eugene would demonstrate a tumble or a backflip and the timing required for a standing somersault, and in no time at all my supple nine-year-old body could make a fair replication of the movement and with a little practice soon perfect it. 'One day I will teach you to fly, little Tamara,' he would laugh. 'To fly without fear and to walk the wire in the sky!'

Of course, when my mother discovered me tumbling about and twisting in the air she was horrified and the young dancing master was immediately dismissed and replaced by an old man with a shiny bald pate and a dark waxed moustache curled up at the ends. I remember the last two centimetres of the moustache was white, and reminded me of a smug cat licking cream. I hated him from the first moment. He spoke French to me all the time, but with a simply atrocious Georgian accent and seemed immensely pleased with himself. I was also strictly forbidden to practise acrobatics, and a single backflip discovered by one of the servants and reported to my mother would result in me being sent to bed without supper.

My mother also saw that Eugene Wilenski was expelled from the Académie de Danse. I saw him by chance a few weeks later and asked him what he would do? He told me he had no alternative but to join the circus or the army as, without a certificate from the academy, he had no qualifications. I was very sad for him, and I told him that one day I would grow up and be rich and I asked him to wait for me. 'I will marry you and look after you and you will teach me to fly!'

He didn't laugh, instead he touched my cheek lightly with the back of his finger, 'Keep practising, kid, and one day we will meet on the highwire and then go to the trapeze and we will fly into each other's arms.'

On my tenth birthday I was given a party, the same sort of party all little rich girls get when they're growing up. I only remember two things about it, though there was one more thing I ought to have remembered and did some time later. But at ten, children do not have the same priorities as adults. However, what I did remember was the cake and the wish I made when I blew out the ten candles set into its lovely thick pink icing.

It was an orange poppyseed cake with layers of

cream and green marzipan and the usual fuss was made when it was time to blow out the candles and make a wish. I took a deep breath and to the raucous cheering and clapping of the invited children and assembled adults I blew all the candles out in a single breath.

'Make a wish! Make a wish!' everyone shouted.

I closed my eyes and suddenly my imagination filled with people, clowns and acrobats, jugglers, dancing ponies, a tiger that snarled and jumped through a flaming hoop, dwarfs, and a magician in a black frock coat and opera hat and cloak just like what my dear papa wore when he went to the theatre. And in my mind I could hear a voice and it was the voice of Eugene Wilenski, my young dancing master, and I looked up and there he stood on a high swaying pole, which almost touched the canvas roof of the circus tent. I saw the highwire strung from the pole to another on the far side of the tent and he was calling for me to join him.

'Come, little Tamara,' he called in my imagination, 'I *must* have you for my partner, you must walk the wire with me and do somersaults in the air!' He stretched out his arms. 'Will you fly into my arms? Shall I wait for you?'

And then there was nothing and I heard myself saying, 'When I grow up I shall join the circus and become a trapeze artist! That is my dearest wish.'

All the adults laughed, except my mother, and when all the guests had gone I was sent to my room without any supper, which was no hardship as I couldn't have eaten another thing anyway. What was not so nice were my mother's instructions to my nanny, an old *babushka* with one rheumy eye and five coarse hairs sticking out of her chin, who was so ancient she had once been my mother's nanny. She mixed a glass of soapy water and made me wash my mouth out, and then made me swallow the last mouthful of soap suds so that I heaved and brought up the orange poppyseed cake, among other things.

The old hag admonished me. 'That will teach you to disobey your mother. You will grow up to be a perfect young lady, it is *compulsory*, then you will marry into the nobility and that is all there is to it!'

'You are not my mother!' I cried.

'I speak for her,' she spat back. 'You will do as your mama says! Only peasants are tumblers and clowns!' She rose and took the night lamp with her, knowing that I was terrified of the dark. I cried myself to sleep.

Children are not given credit for strong emotions and, in my experience, seldom taken seriously. I was in love and I realised that night that while my inexperience had no name for what I felt, I had been in love with Eugene Wilenski, my young dancing instructor, from the age of seven.

Tamara Polyansky pauses and looks around at the group. 'You have all led such hard, dangerous lives, you must think that my story is being childish and I was some spoiled little rich girl. And, of course, you would be right. When I was growing up I never had to think about anything of importance. Nothing in my life represented any danger to myself or those around me. Food and clothes and a warm bed, holidays in France and England, always in the winter, so my father could show his furs. All these privileges I enjoyed without thinking them in the least extraordinary.

'I can see from the slightly indulgent looks on your faces that you think my desire to become a circus entertainer, a trapeze artist, was a child's notion, a little rich girl's fantasy, and would soon be forgotten. Furthermore, the idea of a ten-year-old girl falling absolutely head over heels in love is not new. Puppy love is common enough, and you will no doubt find mine highly amusing.'

I immediately seek to reassure her. 'Tamara, there is no need to be defensive, we are your friends. So far it is a very good story. People like us have never even entered a house like yours!' I think for a moment, 'Well, perhaps the professor, but certainly not somebody like me.'

The others nod in agreement, with the exception of the professor. And, *of course*, Olga Zorbatov, who as a matter of principle would not agree and would naturally want us to think that, because her husband Sergei was a professor of the stars and a confidant of loony members of the aristocracy, she was accustomed to entering such grand palaces.

Anxious to calm her fears, I continue, 'Your life as a child is as strange to us, Tamara Polyansky, as Mr Petrov's childhood in a fishing village on the banks of the Volga would have seemed to you. So far, my dear, we are loving it a lot and also learning new things about you.' I pause and then add, 'So, you can speak French and I must say I have always admired your nice manners.'

'Thank you, Mrs Moses.' Tamara looks at me gratefully and then gives a nervous little laugh. 'I too have to say that, tonight, hearing myself talk of those days in the Crimea and contrasting it with what happened to me, it is almost as strange for me to understand as it is for you.' She sighs. 'Such a long long time ago, and yet not that long!'

'The only significant measurement of time is experience,' the professor says suddenly. 'History does not record routine and only measures birth, disaster and upheaval in the chronology of our lives.'

For once, I think, I understand this point and what's more agree with him. Maybe I'm getting smart in my old age? Though, more likely, with my luck, the professor is getting stupid. But he is correct, the time span of my own life has always been measured by four disasters. One was the year the crops failed and the government confiscated all the food they could find in the Jewish *shtetls* to give to those Russians who were not Jews. I remember how all the old people in our village deliberately starved themselves to death so that what food we could find would keep the young ones alive. Then there were three Cossack raids, the last one you know about, and of course it was the worst of all. Only I remained with any time left on the disaster calendar of life.

Everything I ever think about starts and finishes with these four disasters. Or what the professor calls upheavals. It is the only measurement I have of my existence on earth. And now, I think to myself, we are about to hear Tamara Polyansky's calendar of upheavals. She who, I beg your pardon, speaks French and has learned English manners so that she should know better than to kiss randy village boys and start maybe a sexual orgy. This is some potential upheaval, disaster, concerning us all which maybe I have personally averted.

'You will recall that I told you of two of my memories of the day of the pink-cake birthday, but there was a third,' Tamara begins, taking up her story again. 'The presence of Count Tolstoy at my birthday party.

'Tolstoy was already an old man and in poor health and had come to live in the Crimea. He had just published his great masterpiece, *Hadji Murad*, and my father, a worshipful and devoted follower, had sent the great Russian genius a sable coat as a gesture of his admiration for the new novel.'

'*Hadji Murad* is the greatest story in the Russian language, in any language, greater even than *King Lear*!' the professor rudely interrupts again.

'I beg to disagree, Professor, Hadji Murad was a tartar, a Muslim, a Chechen from the Caucasian mountains and no friend of the Jews! This much I know of history, also Tolstoy I know, Peter the Great, Catherine, also the Great, but who is this king who wrote a book?'

'No, no, my dear, *King Lear* is a play by William Shakespeare, it is thought by many people to be *the* greatest story ever told!'

Ha! I think, nothing has changed, the professor is just as stupid as before and I am not maybe getting smarter. *Hadji Murad* was a legendary Chechen general under the *imam Shamil* of the Caucasian mountains who fought the Russian Empire in a holy war not so very long ago. Every Russian knows this and also they know Tolstoy, who stands only next to God and the Tsar in the big knows. But who is this *William Shakespeare*? This is someone a person should know?

But, of course, I say none of this. To think is free, to speak can be costly. I'm sorry now that I asked the question, so all I say is, 'That's nice, Professor, maybe some other time this interesting lecture? Tonight, if you would be so kind, we are hearing maybe the greatest story *never* written by Tamara

Polyansky!' I look over at Miss Showbiz, 'I apologise for adding to a certain person's rude interruption, please continue, Tamara.'

'Well, Count Tolstoy must have received my father's gift of the sable coat and it being a pleasant enough, though very cold, day he had put it on and driven over to our estate in a troika. Why, I can only presume, to receive more admiration and adulation from my father, as it was unthinkable that the great man would actually express his gratitude to a fur merchant, a lower member of a society he considered totally corrupt. Count Tolstoy was grateful to no man and it is doubtful he even felt he owed God the least gesture of thanks for granting him the breath of life.' Miss Showbiz laughed, 'Please understand, these are not my own observations but the sentiments I heard expressed about Tolstoy by the writer Maxim Gorky to my father when I was thirteen. After Count Tolstoy's visit my father thought of himself as a bibliophile and began to collect writers. Those he most admired received a fur coat. Gorky's was silver mink.'

Mink, shmink! So much for Mrs Solomon's good coat! I think to myself. Then I look around at our motley group in their badly worn coats. Olga

Zorbatov has a bit of mouldy fox around her collar but there is otherwise no fur to be seen. Mr Mendelsohn's coat is perhaps the best of a bad lot, not counting my own of course. He is holding the baby to his chest under his coat with its dear little head poking out the top of the lapels and both of them are fast asleep.

But back to Tamara's story.

Anyhow, on this afternoon when Count Tolstoy came over to our estate he totally ignored the usual protocol. Tapping his malacca cane on the marquetry floor as though he was blind, and without removing his coat and top hat, he walked straight past the footman and the protesting butler down through the picture gallery and arrived unannounced in the ballroom where my birthday party was taking place.

In fact, he arrived at the very moment I blew out the candles and declared my wish to be a circus acrobat.

'That is an excellent wish, my dear!' Tolstoy declared. 'If more well-born young ladies became acrobats and more acrobats became aristocrats, the Russian nobility would not be the ridiculous circus it has become, and the Tsar not its chief clown.'

He chuckled happily at his own remark, then declared, 'I have thirteen children, all of them born into the nobility, and there is not a decent specimen, not even a good acrobat, amongst them!'

Tolstoy turned to where my father stood and dismissively touched the magnificent sable coat he wore with the tips of his fingers, flicking them away from the soft fur. 'Sir!' he said, almost imperceptibly nodding his magnificent white beard and, at the same time, completely ignoring the presence of my mother who stood thin-lipped beside my astonished and speechless papa.

Tolstoy again addressed me. Scowling at me he said, 'I don't much like children, but that was a fine wish, young lady. Remember, my dear, faith and love require courage and daring.'

Then the old man turned and walked slowly out of the ballroom, through the long gallery, out of the house and was helped into his waiting troika by his manservant, who wrapped a well-worn marmoset fur blanket around his master's knees. He then removed Tolstoy's top hat and placed a Cossack fur hat upon his bald head and wrapped a woollen scarf about the old man's face.

I recall my father still looking completely stunned

and running down the steps, his shoes crunching in the snow and shouting, 'A new fur blanket for the troika, maybe? A little champagne, Master? Some hot beef soup to take on the journey?'

Count Tolstoy removed the scarf from his face. 'Good God, man! Is there no end to your impertinence? I am a *vegetarian*!' Then he wrapped the scarf back over his face, settled into his cocoon of fur, and was off in a snuffling of horses and jingle of sleigh bells.

Whereupon my poor papa was so overcome with gratitude at this visit by the great writer that his eyes brimmed with tears and he started to shake all over, and had to be led back indoors and up the grand staircase on my mother's arm, sniffing and sighing all the way to the bedchamber.

My mama, though, was less impressed by the intrusion. She had been completely ignored and humiliated by a member of the aristocracy and she was very angry. She returned to the ballroom soon afterwards. 'You and your little friends will eat a piece of cake and then they must go home! There is a present for each of them,' she said. Then, calling my old *babushka* nanny over, she whispered into her ear and then looked in my direction and smiled at me. It was a smile I knew well, cold as ice. It was only then that I realised that she was also angry with me, though I could not imagine what I had done to upset her. As I cried myself to sleep that night I thought her anger couldn't possibly be simply because I had made a childish and inappropriate wish, but that it must somehow have something to do with the silly old man who had so rudely interrupted my party.

While Tamara is talking, I look over at the still sleeping Mr Mendelsohn holding Anya's baby in his arms and the infant is now sucking on the top button of his overcoat. I think to myself, how very nice it would be to be a baby snug against my father's breast. Or even to be as contentedly asleep as Mr Mendelsohn himself. All we have heard so far is of pink poppyseed cakes, candles, wishing, circus acrobats, weeping fur merchants and Tolstoy, who everyone knows was a misogynist. Maybe a *babushka* nanny knows something? A little soap in the mouth was not such a bad thing after all. If you don't mind my saying so, from adventure, so far this story goes nowhere not very quickly.

But naturally, all this I say on the inside and on the outside I struggle not to fall asleep! But then, suddenly the story brightens up a bit.

My love for Eugene Wilenski never wavered and nor did my desire to become a trapeze artist and acrobat. Yet I kept my determination to myself so that when I ran away from home at the age of thirteen to join a circus, the wish I had made on my tenth birthday had long since been forgotten by my family.

By this time the Tolstoy visit had been blown up out of all proportion. The collective family memory had become somewhat smudged and the incident was now retold as a visit to my father on *his* birthday (conveniently three days earlier) by the great writer to express his sincere thanks for the sable coat. To hear him speak of it was to presume that my papa and Count Tolstoy were thick as thieves and the occasion a grand banquet, not merely a ten-year-old's silly birthday party.

We were on a business trip to Siberia, where we had travelled part of the way on the Trans-Siberian Railway which was not yet completed, and thereafter by river steamer up the Irtysh River to Omsk where my father had come to bid at a fur auction. By this time Papa was also heavily involved in the wool trade and he had secured a contract to supply overcoats to the Tsar's navy.

Siberia is not a good place to start if you should decide to run away from home. It is filled with vast spaces with not very much in them and a runaway thirteen-year-old girl with a fancy accent and good clothes would soon be noticed. But there was a circus playing in Omsk to which I had been taken. In it was a team of acrobats and trapeze artists who were simply splendid and I made my mind up there and then to become one of them. I had no choice. It was either my father or Eugene Wilenski and I decided I would never fly into my father's arms nor could he walk the highwire with me where heaven begins. At thirteen I was getting almost too old to train as an acrobat. I knew I couldn't leave it a moment longer.

Almost as long as I could remember, my relationship with my mother had been a difficult one, but my father had always indulged me. I would miss him dearly for he had never been unkind to me. Businessmen have little time over for their children, but he liked to have his family with him when he travelled and so I had perhaps seen more of my father than most children of my age. Over the three years that had elapsed since the day of my birthday wish, I had saved all the money my father had given me on various trips abroad and I now had sufficient to pay for my entrance to a circus. All I needed to find was a circus master who wouldn't ask too many questions and agree to take me on.

For a few coins spent at a flea market in Omsk the previous afternoon I had purchased an outfit of secondhand clothes as well as a motley collection of spare bits and pieces to make a change of clothes, which I stored in a battered suitcase.

Dressed in these clothes a casual observer would think I was a cut above a peasant, perhaps the daughter of a minor government official. In fact, I had decided to say that my mother had died of tuberculosis when I was very young and that my father had worked on the building of the Trans-Siberian Railway as an engineer until he had been killed in a cutting explosion. The money I was offering for my tuition was his life savings plus a small accident payment from the Trans-Siberian Railway Company.

Leaving our hotel was simple enough. I had

observed the location of the servants' entrance and had quietly slipped out just after midnight dressed in my secondhand clothes and a white pinafore and cap I had removed from a hotel laundry basket. I was only thirteen, but I had travelled extensively and was well versed in the ways of a grand hotel.

Fate was on my side. I arrived at the circus site at six o'clock on the morning of the day of their departure by river steamer to the small city of Pavlodar in Kazakhstan, about two hundred kilometres away.

It took me two hours before I could persuade any of the circus folk to regard me seriously enough to take me to the circus owner. When eventually I stood before him I seemed to quickly convince him that my story was genuine. He agreed almost the moment he discovered how much money I possessed. Life is cheap in a circus, on the other hand money is everything, so with all of my money in his pocket I instantly became a member of the circus. And, as the professor has so eloquently put it, the first upheaval in my small life began.

Circus life is hard for anyone, and for a little girl who had scarcely tied her own hair ribbons it came as an awful shock. If I had imagined that I would be actually trained by the acrobats in my new life I was quite mistaken. I had to fend for myself from the first day and I was treated as a nuisance and the dogsbody. I cleaned out the animal cages, filled the barrels with sawdust, spread it, swept up, washed the dishes after the acrobats had eaten and, in return, I was allowed a few crusts from their leftovers.

Circus people all work hard and are constantly hungry, and living off leftovers was a very precarious business. In a circus you only eat well when you become useful and useful means being a part of an act. I was taught nothing but learned a lot just by watching and emulating my betters. For the first year while we travelled throughout Kazakhstan I cried myself to sleep every night on my bed of straw under the tiger's cage.

'You slept under the tiger's cage?' Olga Zorbatov exclaimed, clearly astonished. 'The tiger's cage?' she repeated.

Tamara laughed. 'It was safe, smelly but safe,' she looked mischievously around, 'Tiger's piss stinks twenty times worse than a cat's and, besides, the tiger looked after me, she was my friend.'

'You became a tiger trainer?' Olga asked, astonished.

'No, no, I had to clean out its cage and often I would help to feed it, and it got used to me being around.'

'But to sleep under a tiger's cage? In a circus this is normal?' I asked, amazed.

Tamara sighed. 'The only thing that is normal in a circus for a thirteen-year-old is that she is definitely not a virgin. I was pretty and my bumps in front were developing and I had a narrow waist and good legs and . . .'

She stopped, then continued. 'As you know I slept under the tiger's cage. Tigers are nocturnal animals, they prowl all night, up and down the cage. If any person approached, the tiger would snarl long before any of the men could crawl under the cage to get at me. I would always have a timely warning and be able to run off or scream,' Miss Showbiz grinned, 'usually both, and the tiger would get very excited and between me screaming and the tiger snarling and bumping against the bars of its cage the whole circus would be roused. The men who worked in the circus soon gave up and it was two years before I lost my virtue.'

Tamara gave her little laugh again, and I must say I was beginning to respect her. 'In a circus, a fifteen-year-old virgin is practically an old spinster!' she added ruefully.

We were obviously too polite to ask how she did lose her virtue, but I'm sure I wasn't the only one who would have liked to know a juicy bit of information like that. To my surprise she simply told us.

After I had overcome the terrible culture shock, or, as the professor puts it, the upheaval in my life, and believe me, if I could have run away I would have done so every day of the first year in the circus.

But where could I go? We were in the middle of Siberia. I had no money, I had no means of contacting my father, I didn't even have paper and pencil and, besides, I could never have afforded the cost of the postage.

When you occasionally meet someone who has been to prison in Siberia, you will understand how impossible it is to escape. I had sent *myself* to Siberia and I was a prisoner just as much as if I had been locked up every night. I worked twelve, sometimes sixteen hours a day. But somehow I managed to do the acrobatic exercises and practised a little and soon, after my first year and well into my second year, I began to understand the ways of the circus. I started to know what it means to be one of the circus people, how you are different, a separate tribe, a different language, a unique life and, most of all, that there is a price to pay for every skill in the circus, for every chance you are given.

At fifteen, though, I worked hard and never complained, I had nothing to give, nothing to barter, well, that is until the circus owner called me into his caravan one afternoon. We were in Samarkand in Uzbekistan where the people have dark almond-shaped eyes and olive skin and after we had erected the tents and everything was ready for the evening show I was summonsed to appear in front of the great man.

I was quite terrified, the owner was a huge man, a Georgian, with an enormous belly and waxed moustaches like my old dancing master and he was totally bald. Despite his fatness, his power was awesome and he would still occasionally appear in leopard-skin tights as the circus strong man. It was also claimed that he could eat half a goat on his own.

I stood in front of him as he peeled an orange slowly with his grubby thumbnail. His thumbnail was at least six centimetres long and I had heard that it was as sharp as a razor. All the acrobats and the clowns or anyone who he thought was not performing properly knew what it felt like to have his thumbnail jabbed into their backsides until the blood ran.

So there I stood, barefoot and in rags. I was shivering mostly with fear but also from the chill in the air and watched him slowly peel an orange, keeping the skin in one piece. His nail stayed motionless as he slowly rotated the brilliant orange-coloured peel off the luscious fruit.

This process seemed to take a long time and when it was complete and the twist of peel lay like a brightly coloured snake on the table in front of him he looked up. He had blue eyes, icy eyes, hooded like a reptile, so that they never seemed to open entirely, and the blue slits were so sharp and so cold that you felt goosebumps when he looked at you. I had not spoken to him since he had taken all my money nearly two years previously. 'What is your name, child?' he asked.

'Tamara Polyansky, sir,' I stammered, not in the

least surprised that he had forgotten all about me. By this time I was so demoralised that I would have been very surprised if he had even remembered me.

'Oh, yes, the child from Omsk.' His eyes seemed to travel all over my body, then back to me. 'You want to be an acrobat, and work on the trapeze?'

'Yes, sir,' I could hardly breathe and my heart started to pound in my breast but I dared not look at him.

'Are you one of us, now?'

I knew what he meant, was I circus folk? I nodded, my head still bowed.

'For your entire life, Tamara Polyansky?'

'I want nothing else, sir,' I managed to whisper.

'Good' he said. 'You may join the acrobatic troupe. Mitya Pimenov will look after you, she will be your mother.'

'Mother' is a term used in the circus which bears no relationship to the true meaning of the word. There is no mother love involved and no mothering. It means that, in return for being trained, I would virtually be a slave to Mitya Pimenov. There was nothing she couldn't ask me to do and I had not the least right of refusal.

But Mitya Pimenov was the best, she could tumble and fly like an angel and her courage on the trapeze knew no limits. I worshipped her from afar, because she was also very beautiful. But I knew enough about the training to know that she would be remorseless with me and never show me the least hint of kindness.

Female acrobats are bred to be hard. Most know they will die young and that to feel for someone else and then lose them is a cause of an inconsolable grief, bringing with it a fear of flying. High flyers believe that the ghost of the loved one rides the wire. There is even a name given for this departed loved one, male or female, the Witch on the Wire. The superstition is that the loved one will bring about the demise of the one left behind.

'Thank you, sir, I am most grateful,' I stammered again.

There was now a brittle silence between us, mine because I dared not say anything more and his for reasons I couldn't for a moment guess at. Besides, I did not have the courage to glance up at him. Finally the huge man said, 'Look up, child! A trapeze artist is proud, unafraid, even of the circus owner. Look up, Tamara Polyansky, and watch and listen and you will learn something.'

I looked up into those terrible, cold eyes. He was holding the orange and had his thumb pushed into the top of the peeled orb. 'There is an entrance fee,' he said and the thumb rose, then pushed back into the top of the orange and then rose again and was once more pushed down so that some of the juice from within poured up out and over the sides of the orange and onto the surface of the table. The owner reached down and dabbed the pudgy forefinger of his free hand into the liquid and brought it to his mouth. 'The circus owner always gets first taste, Tamara Polyansky. It is a tradition, a circus tradition.' His thumb bore down into the orange a little deeper and suddenly the fruit broke open into two halves. 'What was closed must be opened. If you wish to fly like a bird, little Tamara, then first we must open the cage.' He put his thumb with the sharp nail into his mouth and sucked the juice from it. 'And that is my job. I am the cage opener and I also own the bird within it.'

Tamara shrugs. 'At fifteen I became an acrobat and . . .' She pauses for a moment and whispers, 'also not a virgin any more.'

As Tamara has been speaking she has been systematically unbraiding her hair. I do not think she is conscious of doing this, it is simply a nervous gesture. But now it hangs in a shower of gold on either side of her pretty face.

She brings both her hands up and sweeps the hair back and shakes her head.

I didn't care, I was an acrobat. In my mind I had always been an acrobat and had tumbled and jumped, so that when the time came there was nothing to open, the blood so treasured on the wedding night was long ago lost in some child's acrobatic movement. If there was nothing to open, then there was something to close. The fat circus owner closed the door to my innocence forever.

Again, I gave this no thought. The little rich girl I had been was long dead and innocence in a circus is not a commodity to be treasured. Besides, I now cared only about three things, to walk the wire, to become a trapeze artist and to find Eugene Wilenski. I had convinced myself that he had returned to the circus and was somewhere in Russia.

In fact, the Wilenski family were well known among circus folk. The first flying trapeze to start in Russia in 1864 had a Wilenski as a tumbler and contortionist. Fathers, uncles and cousins were circus folk and it was unthinkable, I told myself, that Eugene would go into the military when he could so easily return to the circus where he was born. I would find him and, when I did, I would fly into his arms and walk the wire of heaven with him.

There is not much more to tell of my circus career in the years that followed. The broken bones, the disappointment, the grinding routines, the constant striving for perfection were simply accepted. Trapeze artists grow old young in a circus. But I became, in circus terms, 'A Master of the Art', a flying trapeze artist and wire walker who would claim top billing on the circus posters.

Tamara Polyansky
The Queen of Heaven
challenges
the Prince of Darkness
to a contest in which
one of them must die!

is what the posters proclaimed. I was dressed as an angel in a brilliant white and blue costume ablaze with silver spangles which showed my figure to perfection, whereas my male counterpart wore jet-black tights and a top with a close-fitting cap around his head with red horns protruding from it and a fiery red arrow-pointed tip on the end of his long tail.

We would fly through the air as though in mortal combat, twisting and tumbling and catching each other. And then when it looked certain that the Prince of Darkness would triumph, I would climb down the trapeze pole to where the highwire stretched and start to walk across it as though escaping. The Prince of Darkness, to a dramatic drum roll, would swing across the circus tent to the opposite side, and then he too would come down onto the wire at the opposite end, clutching a fiery sword. He would move towards me with the music building the tension higher and the lights would dim to a single spotlight which transfixed us on the wire.

The spotlight would gradually diminish as he drew closer and closer, sometimes widening a little as I attempted to walk backwards to escape the flaming sword. I'd pretend that it was hardly possible, giving the audience the impression that I was not good on the wire and was in imminent danger of plummeting to my death.

The audience could see that no net was strung beneath us to catch me and at this stage of the act they were almost hysterically afraid. The dark demon with the flaming sword, so adept on the wire, came nearer and nearer until we reached the centre of the wire, thirty metres above the ring, and the spotlight went out.

Now only the flames from the sword lit the scene and the remainder of the circus was in complete darkness. The Prince of Darkness, with his body crouched low, lunged forward, intending to run me through with the fiery blade.

Whereupon I leapt high and catapulted over his body. The sword thrust, meeting only air, threw the devil completely off balance and he plunged, sword in hand, screaming into the pitch-darkness below. The orchestra stopped in mid-note, seemingly in surprise, and the thud of the devil's body was plainly heard as it hit the ground.

The sword had extinguished itself on the way down and now the audience waited in total darkness. Only a matter of moments later a spotlight came on to reveal the devil dead and lying in a pool of blood in the middle of the ring impaled on his own sword, the bright glint of its blade covered with blood.

Then, to the haunting strains of a lone violin, the spotlight lifted to show me balanced on the wire high above. The Queen of Heaven victorious over the Prince of Darkness. The music swelled to a triumphant climax and the spotlight widened, the orchestra died down until there was only the sound of muffled drums as the clowns, dressed in black, carried the devil's lifeless body from the ring, the sword still skewered through his stomach.

We all begin to spontaneously applaud, that is except the professor.

'Trick lighting, smoke and mirrors!' he says gruffly.

Tamara Polyansky grins and looks over at the professor. 'Most of it, yes. But not the leap over the devil's back. This part of the act required me to jump in the dark and land back on the wire. Though the acrobatics and wire work in the act were truly marvellously done, it was this daredevil ability alone which gave me the coveted title, Master of the Art, and also, by the way, cost me thousands of hours to perfect.'

Tamara now has us completely in her thrall and even Mr Mendelsohn is once again awake and listening, so we are, well I know I am, disappointed when she says, 'Enough of circus. I was at the top of my profession and we played all over Russia.

'It was in St Petersburg, where the usual poster with my face on it was pasted everywhere, that I finally caught up with my mother. She visited me one afternoon at the circus dressed to the nines and wearing a sable fur. She coldly informed me that my father had died of the English influenza and that she had taken over his business.

'"No more silly furs, we now deal exclusively in wool, and supply both the Russian Imperial army and the navy with overcoats," she said and then went on to tell me that she was now married to a count, who was also an admiral in the Tsar's navy. They were, she said, in St Petersburg because her husband was to receive his commissioning patents from Tsar Nicholas to be the admiral responsible for the fleet at Port Arthur. This was where a good part of the Russian fleet stood ready to defend the Tsar's dominion over Manchuria, the vast territory Russia had recently confiscated, stolen would be a better word, from China.

'My mother seemed to relish the meeting between us and lost no time pointing out to me that she had achieved for herself what she had always hoped for her daughter, and was now a countess in her own right.

'She also took some delight in informing me that she had finally persuaded my father that I was dead and therefore he had left me no inheritance and, furthermore, that she was now so well accustomed to the idea of my permanent demise that she never wished to see me again.'

Tamara shrugs, 'I remember how she concluded this last statement. "There is no more room in my life for a clown like your father or a cheap circus acrobat like his daughter," she said as she took her leave. "Goodbye, Tamara, I doubt that we shall meet again, but if we do you will refer to me as Countess Ivanovitch and not as Mother."'

Tamara Polyansky smiles. 'So, that was that, the circus became my only family.'

'Good riddance to bad rubbish, if you ask me,' Olga Zorbatov sniffs, 'You are better off without her, my dear. An unfaithful mother is far worse than an unfaithful lover. The lover you can at least replace!'

It is the first joke we have ever heard from Olga, but I suspect she means it, because when we all laugh she says, 'It's true! I promise you, it's true!' as though she means it.

As for Miss Showbiz? Her slow-starting story has now changed from a trickle into a rushing torrent of interest and now none of us wants her to stop.

'Is that all? Is that the end?' I ask, plainly disappointed. 'So, tell me, please, Tamara. What brings you amongst this group of millionaires and playboys?' I gesture to our group, all of whom laugh except Olga, who, of course, misses the joke.

'By no means the end, Mrs Moses, shall I continue?' Tamara Polyansky says. I think she was delighted that we seemed to be enjoying her newfound talent for telling a story.

You will, of course, know that the Japanese attacked the Russian fleet at Port Arthur in order to take Manchuria from us. Well, on the night of the terrible attack in which most of the Russian fleet was destroyed and with it a great many sailors and soldiers, my mother's husband, the count and admiral, was among those who perished. It just so happened that the circus was also in Port Arthur on that night and by morning we found ourselves prisoners of the Imperial Japanese Forces.

I cannot say why the Imperial Japanese Army, who took over the port after the Russian fleet was destroyed, wanted a circus, but they did.

They made us pack up and we travelled together with a long line of prisoners of war into Manchuria. We were treated well enough at first, and the Japanese soldiers for whom we performed nightly shows seemed to enjoy us equally as much as our own countrymen.

Circus folk will do almost anything for applause and we soon practically forgot that we were consorting with the enemy. After all, any audience is good when it laughs and cries and loves the mime and the tricks and comes back for more. My 'Angel versus the Devil' highlight was soon transformed into a form the Japanese soldiers could understand and it worked just as well as ever. My final leap on the wire would leave the hard-bitten soldiers swooning and gasping and at every performance dozens would faint. I suppose they were only young peasant boys really and they would clap and cheer at the death of the Prince of Darkness who had been transformed in the Japanese version into a wicked demon or spirit.

But one night, a soldier became so emotionally carried away that he ran from his seat to where my partner lay in the centre of the ring with the sword through his body pretending to be dead, and fixing a bayonet to his rifle he repeatedly stabbed the so-called dead body through the heart before he could be pulled away.

But before I go on I have to make a terrible confession. I became the mistress of Colonel Tanaka, the Japanese commandant of the prisoner-of-war camp. I beg you to understand I had no choice, the circus owner was simply told that it was the circus or me. Naturally, I was forced to accept, the circus was my family, and one does not kill one's own family, even though I would have gladly died rather than become the concubine for a Japanese officer.

I was also allowed to stay with the circus and perform and the people in the circus knew I was keeping them alive, so they never mentioned the liaison and were always kind to me. This had happened some time before my partner on the wire was killed by the over-excited soldier.

. . .

'We accept it was not your fault, Tamara,' I said.

'Yes, I would have done the same,' Anya said. 'That is, if I had been brave enough. It was a noble and wonderful thing you did, Tamara Polyansky!'

Tamara wiped her tears with the sleeve of her pretty blue dress, sniffed and acknowledged Anya and myself with a grateful smile, then continued.

When my partner was killed I devised a solo act, but it was not the same. The Japanese soldiers far and wide had heard of 'The Good Spirit Angel wrestling in the air with the Bad Spirit Demon'. There was hardly a soldier in the Emperor's Imperial Japanese Army stationed in Manchuria who would not have given a week's wages to see the act. I was famous and, I suppose, for an occidental, much admired. The Japanese have a great capacity for theatre and make-believe and have an intense love of fantasy and are all very superstitious and believe implicitly in good and evil spirits.

How this next chapter in my story came about I can't say, but one morning Colonel Tanaka rose from the tatami mat where he had made love to me and said that I would have a new partner. I had one month to train him to perform my signature act.

As I laced up his boots he announced, 'You will be perfect in one month! If not, we stop circus and you all die!' He pointed a stubby finger at me. 'Not you, you mine! All others die! Understand?' He spoke to me in French which was the language we used. He had learned it while studying to be an engineer in France.

'Master, your humble servant cannot take just anyone and train him to be an acrobat and walk the highwire,' I said. 'Not in a month, not even in a year!' I pleaded.

'He is already trained. One month, no more!' he shouted. 'He is Russian!' He said this as though, in his mind, all it took to restore the act was to recruit another Russian to be my partner.

'But is he *really* an acrobat? Does he know the highwire?' I begged to know.

'Of course!' With this he walked out of the tiny bedchamber. 'One month!' he bellowed as he retreated into his office.

Later that morning I was summoned to the tent of the circus owner who, since subsisting on a meagre rice diet, had lost considerable weight. I entered his tent to find that a Russian prisoner of war stood nearby. The man had his back to me, but

I could see that what remained of his uniform was in rags. He wore no boots on his feet, though the insignia on his tattered coat sleeve denoted that he was a captain in the Imperial Horse Brigade.

'Colonel Tanaka has informed me that you know of this plan to give you a new partner, Tamara?' The circus owner spread his hands and sighed as if to indicate that while he knew the task was impossible it was up to me and that I must attempt to achieve the impossible.

'But it is not possible! I tell you, it can't be done! This is an act that took two years to perfect! It simply couldn't be done in one month by God's only son Himself!' I said, releasing my anger and frustration in front of the owner.

'I don't know about that. *He* could walk on water, Tamara Polyansky,' came the voice from the man in rags. He turned and I found myself staring into the emaciated face of Eugene Wilenski! He reached out and with the back of his index finger lightly brushed my cheek. 'Keep practising, little nanotchka, and one day we will meet on the highwire, and then go to the trapeze where we will fly into each other's arms.'

Of the next month, what can I say? I have never

worked so hard in my life. Eugene was a natural but he was rusty and his muscles unaccustomed to doing acrobatic work, and besides he was half starved. At least I was able to get the colonel to put him on a good diet and he ate voraciously to gain the strength he needed for the work at hand.

The first performance a month later was nothing to shout about, but we muddled through it and the Japanese soldiers seemed not to see the many glaring imperfections in the act. In six months we were nearly perfect. Eugene was a marvel and as I flew nightly into his arms high above the screaming soldiers I fell more and more deeply in love. I had always loved only him but now my whole body and soul ached to have him. At night when I lay with the colonel I imagined it was Eugene and fantasised that we had escaped and were passionate lovers and would eventually die in each other's arms.

Once Eugene Wilenski no longer saw me as a child he too began to love me, although slowly at first. There was so little time to be kind and he had so much to learn and I was often forced to be stern, even to shout at him. Russian men, especially men from the Crimea, do not like their women to be assertive. But in the end I do not believe he could help himself and he declared his love for me.

We could never consummate our love, for if it was discovered I felt sure we would both be executed. I also learned that Colonel Tanaka had found Eugene by promising that if any Russian prisoner of war was by chance a trapeze artist who could walk the highwire and would agree to come forward, for every act he completed in the circus, the life of a Russian prisoner of war would be spared.

It was of course a long shot on the colonel's part but it worked. Every day five Russian prisoners were executed as a matter of routine. It was called the Lottery of the Dead, the five prisoners were selected by the colonel simply at random as he inspected the ranks each morning. Now there was this seemingly miraculous chance to save one lottery winner each day, and so Eugene had come forward. Our act had literally become a matter of life or death. And, if we were discovered to be lovers, a great many Russians would die as a consequence.

We worked together for one year and three days. Despite the circumstances, I must tell you I am not ashamed to say they were the happiest days of my life. To have been so loved that every nerve end in your body responded was like being in the presence of angels.

I would fly gleefully through the air and we would do more and more impossible figurations until, I do believe, Eugene and I were possibly the finest aerial act in the world. And always as we performed and my body twisted with his own in the air we were consciously making love, fantastic love. Frequently at the end of a breathless movement I felt myself grasped in his strong arms, and no consummation between two lovers could ever have been better wrought nor satisfied more. We were making glorious and beautiful love in the air and below us the soldiers were entranced with what they regarded as the eternal battle between good and evil.

When, in the end, I leapt over Eugene's lunging body and flaming sword and stood high on the wire to look down at him spotlighted in the ring lying in the pool of fake blood with the fake sword through his back, all I saw was a beautiful lover, exhausted from making love to me in the air and on the heavenly wire.

And then on the evening of the fourth day of the second year Eugene and I were together, on a night seemingly no different to any other, Colonel Tanaka attended our performance.

The show opened in the usual way, and as always our act was the grand finale. The only difference was that instead of dedicating our performance to a colonel, general or captain of whatever regiment was attending the performance that night, I dedicated it to Colonel Tanaka. I stood high up on the trapeze and in Japanese, for I now had a reasonable grasp of the language, I made the dedication.

My enemy lover stood up where he sat with the other officers and formally saluted. He was in his dress uniform with shining knee boots and he wore a dress sword as well as his service revolver. He seemed very pleased as he bowed towards me and I bowed in return from the trapeze high above his head. The troops all cheered their heads off and we were off to a grand start.

I knew that the dedication had been a popular success and that Colonel Tanaka had gained great face and that I had greatly honoured his presence in a most appropriate manner. I could sense Eugene's amusement as he stood in the dark on the trapeze platform at the other side of the tent, no doubt grinning to himself and hopeful that my gesture of respect might save all five of tomorrow's lottery winners. I had promised him that if the colonel was pleased with the show I would attempt to persuade him to save all the next morning's lottery winners as a gesture of goodwill.

If anything our performance that night was more brilliant than it had ever been. We had reached the finale on the wire after our technique on the swings had been faultless. Now Eugene, with the flaming sword in hand, advanced towards me and I, with feigned uncertainty, attempted to walk backward on the wire to escape my determined assailant. Eugene, for his part, stalked me with a panther-like ease, the spotlight bringing us closer and closer together, the tension building. Then, at the precise moment the music stopped and only the flames from the moving sword lit the scene, a single shot rang out.

The bullet caught Eugene in the chest halfway through the movement of the sword thrust. I saw a brilliant scarlet spray of blood as the vicious bullet ripped open Eugene's chest and he fell backwards away from me and plunged wildly downwards, missing the small net positioned in the darkness which was intended to break his fall. I instinctively jumped over him as he fell from the wire and the circus tent went into total darkness as the sword extinguished. I landed back on the wire in the dark and held my balance. There had been two thuds in the three seconds it took him to fall. Moments later the spotlight came back on, but Eugene did not lie in his accustomed spot in the centre of the circus ring, though I could clearly see the pool of fake blood prepared for his body. The spotlight swayed, then moved left and then right and forward again across the ring until it found his broken body and held still.

The soldiers were yelling and screaming their heads off, thinking it all a part of the act. Suddenly Colonel Tanaka walked into the spotlight and stood beside Eugene's broken body. Slowly he drew his sword and with a fierce, sharp shout he raised the samurai sword above his head and, using a double-handed grip on its haft, he swiftly brought it down, the blade whipping in the air before separating Eugene's head from his torso.

There is a gasp and then a soft moan to my left and Olga Zorbatov slumps beside me into a dead faint. Anya and Mitya Shebaldin both have their hands up to their faces and Mr Mendelsohn breaks down and weeps. For my part, while deeply shocked, I've seen the Cossacks do the same thing in my village and am probably the first to compose myself.

Tamara is now weeping loudly and I rise, taking her into my arms, 'Sshhh! We will help you, we are your friends, Tamara,' I say, rocking her like a baby in my arms. It is not much, but soon her tears and gulps quieten and after some time she draws herself away from me and needlessly apologises to us all.

In the meantime we've all forgotten about poor Olga Zorbatov, but like a true Taurus, she gives a sudden bellow and promptly recovers from her faint. To be born under the sign of the bull is not easy, nobody seems in the least concerned for her.

'It is enough for one night,' I say.

But Tamara's hand rises to still me. 'Please, Mrs Moses, I do not possess the strength to go through this again another night.' She looks around, her eyes taking us all in. 'With your kind permission I would like to complete my story.'

Then Tamara Polyansky tells us how Colonel Tanaka has discovered her love for Eugene.

· · ·

One night, the circus owner had become uproari-
ously drunk on *sake*, Japanese rice wine, during a
reception after a particular circus performance.
Hoping to ingratiate himself, he had whispered into
the ear of a visiting infantry captain that the two
high-flying trapeze artists were lovers. The
infantry captain, thinking little of this information,
had mentioned it in passing to another officer and
eventually it had been told to Colonel Tanaka.

Colonel Tanaka now waited for me to come
down from the highwire and dragged me by the
hair towards the owner's tent.

'You have been unfaithful!' he screamed in
Japanese. 'You must pay with your life, whore!'

'Kill me! I beg you to kill me!' I shouted back.
'Do it now, shoot me now!' I sobbed.

Instead he threw me inside the tent where the
circus owner cowered in the corner on his knees.
He crawled, whimpering, on his knees towards
Colonel Tanaka and commenced to beg for mercy,
sobbing and then kissing the toes of his shiny dress
boots.

Tanaka released his grip on my hair and I too fell
to the ground but then leapt up again. 'Kill me, you
bastard!' I screamed, attacking him with my nails.

Tanaka knocked me down with the back of his hand, but I rose again just as he drew his revolver and shot the circus owner through the back of the head.

'You!' he screamed in French at me. 'For you, something worse than death!'

I was sent to northern Japan where I became a comfort woman in a brothel for soldiers. There I would often be used a hundred times a day. If I had not been constantly watched I would have taken my own life a dozen times. In 1910, during the course of a small earthquake when the brothel was totally disrupted and the guards were running for their lives, I escaped. Eventually I crossed the La Perouse Strait to the Russian island of Sakhalin and told my story to the military authorities.

But I found that I was no heroine. Instead I was wanted by the Tsar's secret police as well as the military authorities. The military wanted me for consorting with the enemy, and the secret police for being a spy against Imperial Russia.

Because the secret police had precedence over the military and were besides a huge and somewhat befuddled bureaucracy, it was somehow necessary for me to be interrogated in Moscow several thousand kilometres away. The military declared that they would have saved the Tsar the expense and simply taken me out and shot me while, at the same time, resenting the cost of a bullet for the little yellow man's whore.

I will spare you a description of the journey by boat and then by train across Russia. There are few miseries as great. But after several weeks, when it became apparent that I had no interest in escaping and didn't seem to much care whether I lived or died, my guards removed the shackles from my wrists and ankles so that I could prepare their food and do other duties, including the one I had been doing for the Japanese soldiers. The uniforms may change but what's below the belt of a man who has power over a woman remains constant.

We were in the final stages of our journey to Moscow and I had long reconciled myself to the fact that I was going to die and, in a perverse sort of a way, I welcomed the fact that the Tsar's secret police would make my death a long and painful one.

I did not believe I had a right to live. Too many people had died because of me. Eugene, all the circus folk, and hundreds of prisoners of war who might otherwise have been saved if I had not loved Eugene so much.

I believed I wasn't worthy of the gift of life. That the life in me must be ripped from my abused and worthless body to expiate my sins, my terrible crimes against my countrymen.

We were perhaps a day's journey from Moscow and it was late at night when we came to a halt at an obscure railroad station with the name of Astapovo. It was so small and remote that my guards allowed me to alight and fetch fresh water and to wash out the samovar in which I brewed their tea.

The train was to stop at the larger town of Tula further down the track, but we were getting close enough to Moscow for my guards to want to take the precaution of replacing my shackles. Not that they thought I would escape, but because they might be seen to be careless in their duties. Tula was much too large a centre to let me fetch water.

It was cold, late autumn, November cold, when the wind starts to come in from the north. I wore only a threadbare kapok coat over a coarse linen dress and on my feet peasant sandals made of hemp. I entered the small shack on the platform which was no more than a hovel and from which came a dim light. If it was occupied I thought I might enquire about water, ask where the well was situated, since most railway stations have a well close by. In the corner, lit by a tiny oil lamp of the kind a traveller might use, lay an old man. He was gasping and wheezing and seemed to be in terrible distress. But I hardly noticed. Beside him was a small suitcase and a large vacuum flask, which I hoped might contain something warm to drink. If the old man was too frail or sick to answer my request for the where-abouts of the well, I was beyond caring that he seemed to be dying. I had seen so much death that, had I thought about it, I would have resented the old man's tenure on life. His time was up and he had no further right to the flask beside him.

I slowly approached him and stretched my hand out to take the flask when he looked at me. I was close enough to touch him. My hand paused, leaving the flask where it stood. The old man was Leo Tolstoy, the great writer.

I knew this with absolute certainty. The mis-shapen nose, high brow, bald head, his piercing blue eyes now somewhat dimmed, and, of course, the great white beard. What made me certain though was the sable coat he wore. It was the coat my father had given him. Old peasant men do not die in sable coats. I knew it was Tolstoy as sure as I know the nose on my face.

I lifted him into my arms, he was surprisingly frail and even through the lustrous fur coat I could feel his sharp old bones.

'Count Tolstoy, I would consider it a great honour if you will let me help you,' I heard myself saying in the accent of my former well-bred self.

'Child, I am dying, there is nothing you can do for me but report it to the authorities.' He seemed to smile and then continued. 'Who, I feel sure, will report it to the Tsar and to the Church, both will be pleasantly pleased to hear the news of my demise and will perhaps call for some positive verification, a lock from my beard perhaps, or a finger for future reliquiae of the devil himself?'

'I met you at my tenth birthday party, master. You came to our house to . . .' I stopped. 'Well, I'm not sure I know why you came, sir?'

For a moment a gleam came into his eyes. 'Ah, the birthday girl who wanted to be an acrobat. How did it go?'

'It went well, sir,' I said smiling. 'Very well.'

'That's right, my child, never let them get the better of you. Not until your final breath. Never give up! Damn the Tsar, damn his eyes and his soul, may he rest in an unmarked grave!' With these words he slumped back in my arms.

I let him down gently and rushed out of the small hut. 'It's Tolstoy, Count Leo Tolstoy, he is dying in there!' I cried and pointed to the railway hut.

Of course, at first, the people on the train thought I had gone crazy. But I kept running up and down and yelling until a reluctant train inspector alighted and then another official followed him and, when they entered the hut and didn't immediately return, more people crowded around, until the entire train spilled out onto the tiny platform and beyond. Someone with more credibility than I positively identified Tolstoy, no doubt having seen his picture or perhaps the contents of his small suitcase. As I remember, there were almost as many pictures of him in Russia as there were of Tsar Nicholas.

'It is Tolstoy, he is dying!' people were shouting and running around. They were shocked but also secretly consumed by excitement and pride though trying not to show it. They knew they were eye witnesses to history, to a national tragedy, news that would shake Russia to the core and spread like a whirlwind around the world.

It was then that I quietly slipped into the night. I had just taken advice from the greatest intellect Russia has ever produced, a man acknowledged by Russians to be the greatest writer in literature. If he said I was not yet ready to surrender, who was I to argue?

Tamara smiles and spreads her hands and looks over at me.

'And then one day I found you, Mrs Moses, who will lead us through the wilderness to the promised land.'

News of Tolstoy's collapse in the obscure railroad station of Astapovo, one hundred and sixty kilometres to the southeast of Moscow, was spread along the telegraph wires throughout Russia and the world. After he was discovered, Tolstoy lay dying for several days in the little railway station, finally passing away on the 26th of September, 1910, with the world's newsreel photographers recording his death. He refused absolution from the Church or visits from representatives of the Tsar and would not even see his wife, with whom he had quarrelled incessantly to the very end.

CLEOPATRA'S CAT
AND THE
LETTERS FROM EGYPT

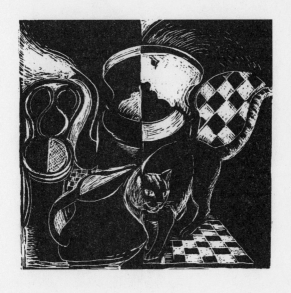

What can I tell you about Mrs Shebaldin? She is a newcomer, a recent addition to our little half-starved journey into freedom. There is not much required to join us, we ask few questions and are not concerned with religion.

Jew, Christian, Muslim, it is all the same, because when you are hungry and frightened the God you choose is important only to yourself. The only prerequisite for travelling with us is that you must be able to walk. So when Mrs Shebaldin told us that she was a foot doctor we ceased immediately to be curious, never mind the fancy questions, a foot doctor is a gift from a loving God.

Like the professor who never quite made the entire journey to Siberia, and Tamara who sent herself there, Mrs Shebaldin also has a story to tell of the desolate wasteland with the name that comes cold and dead to the lips.

Siberia, if you say it slowly, is a malicious word, like a blunt knife pushed slowly into the stomach. It is a landscape filled with dread, a howling gale in the Russian imagination. It is the foul breath of the universe, an endless stench of dark landscape and permafrost where there is no joy, no warm blood, nor kind earth nor sun for the spawning of happiness.

Siberia is where the air itself is the prison guard. It has long been the place the Tsars have sent Russia's so-called enemies, the land where the secret police bury their victims alive in the remorseless tundra and so turn good, strong men into the walking dead.

When a judge condemns a man to be sent to Siberia it is not unusual that he allows the prisoner to return first to his village to attend his own funeral and get drunk at his wake. The judge knows that the Gulag is a one-way trip and every man is entitled to say farewell to his family and kiss his own life a fond goodbye.

These men sent to the slave camps and the salt

mines form the legions of the forgotten, their families mourn them and then they fade from memory. A wife, if she is still young and strong, will marry again and children will talk of a father on whose knee they once sat but who is now long departed.

In Siberia the gates of the slave camps stay open. Only a minimum of guards are required and fewer still in the salt mines. These are dull men who will beat you senseless if you don't work but will invite you to leave any time you may care to do so. 'Be my guest, my friend. Tonight? But of course! You've had enough? Well done! Freedom? Certainly, sir, let me show you to the front gate.' They will turn to the slave next to you. 'This is your lucky day, tonight you shall have his tin of hot water which bears the grand name of soup.'

To escape in Siberia is to die alone and there is nothing a person fears more than that his exit from life will take place unremarked and unmarked. It is unbearable for a man to think of his spirit rising into the screeching wind sucked up into the midnight maw of uncaring space without acknowledging the benediction with the last of his breath.

A man has every right to fear that his soul will lose its way in the vast loneliness, that the howling of the *dybbuk*, his ghost, will be added to the fury of the winter gales. Who will wait with you so that he might cover your silent mouth and close your eyes while, at the same time, steal the gold ring from your finger as a keepsake, to mark your passing?

The professor tells us a story. He is on his way to Siberia, thirty men in a cattle truck, a hundred trucks, transporting three thousand prisoners. The only sounds day after day are the *clickity-clack* of the wheels and the *puff* and *huff* and labour of the hot black engine half a kilometre ahead.

After a week, the men who huddle together against the bitter cold seldom talk. The conversation between them is long exhausted, lives have been explained, laid bare, similarities explored, experiences shared, coincidences examined, connections made, alliances considered. All this and more, until the bones of past relationships have been picked white and discarded. It is now every man for himself as compassion and hope die in the breasts of each of them.

Now there is only the rock and sway of the cattle trucks and the *click* and *clack* of steel wheels beneath their feet. They yearn for a little comfort and put great store in the added warmth to be gained from huddling together against the biting cold.

Occasionally a fight breaks out, a pathetic squabble, like two stray dogs over an old bone as one prisoner tries to snatch a warmer place from a weaker man who may be fortunate enough to lie his cheek against someone who wears a fur coat or a collar of silver fox.

The train stops for twenty minutes every two days to take on water and coal. It is usually snowing and the temperature is below freezing, minus thirty, maybe even more. The engine grinds to a halt, a screaming and whining of metal on frozen rails and a fuss of escaping piston steam. The doors to the trucks are opened and prisoners are let out to defecate.

The professor continues his story and he apologises for the coarse language he feels he must use, explaining that to use words other than 'piss' and 'shit' would alter the sense of what happened.

We nod for him to continue. He is not a man with a dirty mouth and is easily the most educated amongst us, besides, these not-so-nice words we all know exist and so we nod the go-ahead, accepting a suspension of good manners for the necessity of an honest telling of the story.

But, of course, Olga Zorbatov brings her finger

and thumb to clasp her nose, the usual exception to our accord.

'The men learn quickly that when you piss you do not remove your trousers. You simply micturate where you stand, the warm urine running down the inside of your trouser legs. Remove your trousers and the piss freezes in the air, an arc of golden ice that drills back and stabs into the urethra, the penis, the pain of which is said to be indescribable.

'To defecate is not so bad, the trousers may be lowered if the hands are cupped tightly over the genitals to keep them warm. The buttocks may start to freeze but they contain sufficient fat to protect them and the faecal matter within will still drop and the trousers restored in time.'

I now see why the professor has to use common words, after all, the ones he uses to replace them, 'micturate' and 'faecal material', are most complicated and don't sound a bit like what people do, you know, when they have to go.

'By the time the cattle trucks have been opened, the men have about ten minutes to do their business. Both sides of the railway lines are beaded with hundreds of men squatting with their trousers around their ankles. A few have walked away from the side of the trucks, mostly city folk of the better class who are too modest to do their business in public.

'The whistle blows and the train immediately starts to move away, there are only moments left to scramble back into the trucks. Most of the men make it, but those who strayed from the line are seen frantically running to reach their own truck, calling out desperately. They are urged on by the calls of their comrades, who have their hands stretched out to help them aboard, for if they miss boarding the truck to which they belong no other will take them on board.

'But now comes the cruel joke. Those who were too modest to squat beside the rail are generally the ones too shy to clasp their genitals in public. The genitals are the warmest place on the body and when your hands are enclosed around the scrotum your fingers are prevented from freezing. Now as the train pulls away they rise, only to discover that their hands are frozen and they cannot pull their trousers up. So they struggle to hold them up with the sides of their arms while they run, but when they stretch their hands out to be helped aboard, the trousers drop to their ankles and they trip, ploughing into the dirty snow beside the track. There is only hapless laughter from those safely aboard. A man running after a departing train with his trousers falling slowly down around his ankles is very funny even if it is also terribly sad. Tragedy and laughter are twin brothers in Siberia.

'With the mirth of his comrades ringing in his ears a man will pick himself up, but by now the engine is gaining speed and so he stands bare-arsed in the snow helplessly watching his own life disappearing from sight.

'At each coaling stop half a dozen men are left to die in the wind and the blinding snow. A black smudge of engine smoke against the pewter-coloured sky is their last tenuous connection with the living. Good friends, the milch cows coming into the village at sundown, the sharp cries of mothers scolding their children, hot soup, the sound of laughter coming from a lighted tavern, the memory of a first, late-summer mating with a blue-eyed, flaxen-haired maiden in a rustling cornfield, the mewling of a newborn infant – all this is lost forever in the smoke that slowly spreads and fades against the eyeless horizon.'

The professor looks up and opens his hands

wide and sighs, 'What more can I say? That is the train to Siberia.'

Mrs Shebaldin looks up and also sighs, then she says, 'I have spent the last five years of my life in Siberia but I too have never been there. I have been living in Egypt.'

For riddles we haven't got time, I think to myself. Whatever does she mean? Ten years in Siberia but she hasn't been there but also she's been in Egypt, all apparently at the same time? Some people should maybe learn a little more commonsense!

'My husband was a doctor, a famous surgeon,' Mrs Shebaldin explains. 'We lived in a fine house in St Petersburg, near the Academy of Medicine in the Nevsky Prospekt. Uri was a modernist, a Deep Knife, which is what they call the young surgeons at the academy, the older ones have no interest in what lies deeper under the skin but only in what they could chop off.

'"Why leave in what is harmful and will do further harm when it may be neatly cut out and stitched?" my husband would say. "An ulcer will not cure itself nor, for the most part, an abscess on the bowel drain away." He was also a confirmed follower of Charles Darwin. "Nature doesn't always take care of the redundant pieces, we evolve and change but so slowly that there are parts of the human physiology which became unnecessary. When these give trouble they must be removed."'

'Which parts are those, Madam Shebaldin?' the professor challenges.

'Professor, I am not a scientist like you, but my husband talked mostly of internal parts of which I know little, though he did once mention that a man does not need a beard or a foreskin.'

'Bah! Ridiculous! In Siberia he will need a beard and wish also he could grow hair on his nose!'

'And a foreskin, Professor?' I ask, 'We Jews have found it unnecessary to have such a thing for more than a thousand years.'

The professor bows his head towards me. 'With the greatest respect, a small religious ritual, no more, Mrs Moses. I dare say we could smell as well without the tip of our nose but this does not suppose we should cut it off!'

I have never thought of it in quite this manner and I am somewhat shocked that such an essential ritual in the Jewish faith should be dealt with so logically. The professor has a point and certainly I am not prepared to argue with such a learned man. 'Hygiene. It is for hygiene,' I say, not really certain that this is correct.

'In the Arabian desert maybe, in the wilderness where there are sandstorms and sand grit may get under the foreskin to irritate, start maybe an infection. In Russia? I think not, madam.'

'Internal parts, Professor. My husband spoke of internal parts that would benefit from removal with the knife,' Sophia Shebaldin comes to my rescue.

The professor turns to face her. 'I should like to know these parts, Madam Shebaldin. In my experience the removal of any piece of the human anatomy is not without some cost, even if it is deemed necessary.'

'My husband spoke in particular of the tonsils and the appendix,' Mrs Shebaldin says and then to our surprise she suddenly bursts into tears.

'Whatever have I said to upset you, Madam?' the professor cries in alarm.

'Not you, Professor,' Sophia Shebaldin sniffs. 'It is the thought of an appendicectomy.'

'You are crying for the appendicectomy?' the professor says, clearly confused.

Sophia Shebaldin wipes the tears from her eyes.

'The first appendicectomy operation to be performed in Russia, it was the cause of my tragedy, our eventual downfall,' she sniffs again.

She is not the crying type nor even the sort of person you would know how to properly comfort in a weeping situation. Sophia Shebaldin is a thin woman who seems to be composed of sharp edges and hard flat places. Narrow-chested, high-shouldered, legs like knotted twigs on tiny feet, skin stretched taut over her face, a reserved person who seems not to encourage familiarity, though I should add, her expression is never foreboding or unwelcoming. There is simply no fuss to her. Even her grey hair is smoothed and pulled so tightly back into a bun that it gives less the impression of hair than of helmet fashioned in steel. And her hands are long and thin, not beautiful like Mr Mendelsohn's. It is as though her fingers and palms contained no flesh, only a layer of skin to hide the bones beneath.

Only when she massages your tired feet, or works on a painful corn or drains a blister or gently rubs a sprained ankle do you know immediately that these are special hands, the hands of a true healer. She lays them on a painful place and those long, bony fingers seem to pluck the pain from the muscle or the bruise, as though indignant that it should be there. In an hour or two you are ready for the road again.

Of all the people in our little group we can least afford to lose, that is to say, after Mr Petrov of course, it is surely the quiet and unassuming Mrs Shebaldin. But when you thank her for what she does with those remarkable hands she appears embarrassed, 'Tch! It is nothing, only a little massage, any person with a bit of commonsense could do it.'

Because she so easily dismisses our praise, we have, perhaps mistakenly, never seen her as the emotional type, not the sort of person to have a lively imagination. Now we wait for her to explain the tragedy of the appendicectomy.

She looks up at the professor as she speaks. 'You will perhaps recall that the English king, Edward the Seventh, who is cousin to Tsar Nicholas, received the first operation on the human appendix the very day before his coronation was to take place. It was a desperate measure by the royal surgeon Sir Frederick Treves and it saved the king's life.'

The professor nods, though I am not sure that,

like the rest of us, this is not news to him as well. Russia and England are not friends at that moment and not much is heard about the English people that is complimentary. For my part I am not even sure what is this appendix that nearly killed the English king.

'Not so fast if you please, Sophia,' I say. 'What is this appendicectomy?' The others nod agreement, I was right to ask.

Mrs Shebaldin goes to answer when Professor Smarty-Pants says, 'A blind tube projecting from the rounded end of the large intestine.'

How does he know this stuff? This professor of bird calls and numbers?

'So?' I say again, spreading my hands, 'Tell me, please, what does this tube that can't see actually do?' This is the first time I have heard that there are tubes in my body that have eyes.

'Blind means it goes nowhere, does nothing useful, the appendix is a vestigial organ with no function in humans.'

'Ha!' says Olga Zorbatov, 'So Mrs Shebaldin's husband is correct, it is a human part that is no use at all!' She looks pleased that the professor has been caught out.

Mrs Shebaldin on the other hand does not change her expression, she is not interested in playing tricks with the professor or in being proved to be right in the first place.

'Just a little wormlike thing located on the lower right of the stomach,' she says, touching a spot on her lower abdomen and at the same time showing us she knows just as much as the professor without having to gloat like Olga Zorbatov who knows nothing about appendix, worms and tubes, blind or otherwise.

'A little worm that's blind and does nothing, so what's the problem please?' I can see that again I am not the only one who thinks this is a good question.

The professor goes to answer, his mouth is half open, but I hold up my hand. 'I think we are forgetting who is telling this interesting story already, Professor.'

I nod to Sophia Shebaldin. It is a good night, we have a little horse meat and fresh vegetables and potatoes, everything is cooking along nicely and the smells coming from the frying pan are making our stomachs growl. If Sophia Shebaldin's story can get under way maybe we can eat soon.

'It, this little worm, can become infected and

cause inflammation and terrible pain and even burst, and a person with appendicitis may die,' Sophia says. 'They were trying to drain the infection from the English king but the pain and the cramps grew more severe and on the night before his coronation, fever, vomiting and diarrhoea threatened to kill him. Sir Frederick Treves, the royal surgeon, decided to operate, to open him up and drain the infection on the spot and so history was made. Maybe it was not the first appendix operation, who can say for sure, but it was the first on a king and so naturally everyone says it is the first on anybody. And the news spread around the world, even to Russia who was not speaking to England.'

'Schish! What an expert!' is all I can say about Sophia Shebaldin. An expert who knows about a king's personal operations. I can see that even the professor is impressed.

'So?' I say, 'Tell us more if you please.'

Well, my husband Uri and all the other surgeons at the academy hear soon enough about this kingly operation and suddenly it is appendix this and appendicectomy that and appendicitis something else. Every peasant who comes along with a stomach ache they want to open up and cut out his little worm. And then one night, very late, long after we have gone to bed, comes a knock at the door of our house. It is a footman from the palace of Prince Felix Youssopov and he has a note from a physician who is well known among the nobility. The note asks for Uri to come to the prince's palace at Dvortsovaya Ploshchad at once, and to bring his surgical instruments with him.

It is nearly two o'clock in the morning when Uri arrives and he is taken immediately to a bedchamber where a small girl is lying. She is maybe eight years old and he is informed that she is the prince's favourite niece and also related to the Tsar and must be saved.

Uri goes into consultation with the physician, who is convinced that the child has appendicitis. She has a high fever, cramps in the area around the right hip bone and navel, frequent nausea and vomiting, and she is in great pain. The child has been sick for several days and in the last two hours has become unconscious. The fear is that she is dying and it is clear that she cannot be moved. The physician wants Uri to conduct an emergency operation right there in the palace. Everything has been made ready in the kitchen, surfaces have been scrubbed and disinfected, water is boiling and extra lamps have been brought in to aid the operation.

Uri is reluctant, he belongs to the new school of hygiene and the palace kitchen is not suitable for complete sterilisation and, besides, he has not personally conducted an appendicectomy before. The little princess has a pulse rate which is dangerously low and he is reluctant to give her chloroform, which in these conditions could quite easily have stopped her heart.

'You *must* operate!' the famous physician insists. 'This is no different to the English king. The prince will not forgive you if she dies!' He pauses and rubs his beard. 'The Youssopov family has eighty grand estates all over Russia and is second in power only to the Tsar himself.' He fixes Uri with his monocle. 'What kind of career do you imagine you will have at the Academy of Medicine?' He nods his head towards the unconscious child. 'That is to say if the little princess should die without an attempt to save her?' He seems to squint even harder through the glass eyepiece, 'On the other hand, if the child should live, a professor of surgery is not out of the question.'

Uri performed the operation but they had called him in too late, and as the infection had spread to the abdominal cavity the princess died two days later of peritonitis. The first appendix operation performed on a royal personage in Russia had failed.

The news of the little princess's death was carried by the newspapers and the comparison was naturally made with the English surgeon, Sir Frederick Treves. He had managed to save a king. A great scandal was in the making and the court gossips eagerly pointed out that whereas an English king had been saved, a Russian surgeon couldn't even manage to save a small princess who belonged to relatively minor royalty. The papers lamented that Russia, the Tsar and the powerful Youssopov family had been disgraced and humiliated. A scapegoat was needed and Uri was arrested as a clandestine Bolshevik seeking to destroy the throne and sentenced to five years in the salt mines in Siberia.

Being a man of otherwise good character the judge allowed Uri to return home for the banquet of farewell. Or, as it is known by the lower orders and country people, the Feast of the Dead. For this, an open coffin is brought by pallbearers into the prisoner's house and, at one stage during the festivities, he is made to lie in his own death box. The village priest says the prayers for the dearly departed over his live body, whereupon the guests drink a toast of vodka to his future memory.

The banquet of farewell held for Uri was a less bizarre affair, but nevertheless his colleagues from the Academy of Medicine, those who were not too frightened to attend, and our friends and relations scarcely harboured any more hope for his safe return than a peasant family might a convicted son or father. Siberia was a one-way ticket, the cattle trucks were known to always return empty.

Finally the time came for Uri to bid our little family, myself and our two little girls, goodbye. It was a terrible moment for we were very much in love and he doted on Tanya and little Anna. The death of the princess had caused him a great deal of personal distress. The little girl had been the same age as Tanya our eldest. The thought that it could have been Tanya or her younger sister who had died had caused my husband to accept with equanimity his bitter sentence. Somehow, he felt himself to blame, even though both professors of surgery at the academy, called in at the autopsy, had testified to the judge that all the evidence indicated that the surgeon's knife had come too late to save the child, and that peritonitis was well advanced before incision was made and had been the certain cause of her death.

But then the sentence never was about right or wrong, neglect or otherwise. It was about Russia being made to seem inferior to the hated English, that the 'so-called' brilliant young surgeon Uri Shebaldin, unlike the British Sir Frederick Treves, was not up to scratch, or a Bolshevik, or both. It is from such childish notions that the diplomacy of nations is constructed and national pride is gained or lost.

I confess that at our final parting I shed bitter tears and did not behave in the least well. Little Anna, not yet six years old, seeing my distress, crawled onto her father's knee. 'Why are you leaving us, Papa?' she asked. 'Why is Mama crying so?'

Uri, barely able to contain his own grief, kissed the top of her head and then also drew Tanya to his side and held her against him. 'I am going to visit the Queen of Egypt,' he said. 'She has a beautiful daughter just like you and Tanya, only your hair is fair and your eyes are blue. Her little girl has hair black as midnight and eyes the colour of jade.'

'What's her name?' Anna asked.

'Who? The Queen of Egypt or her daughter?'

'The queen's name is Cleopatra, silly!' Tanya said to her younger sister. 'Everyone knows that!'

Anna, not to be outdone, shot back, 'I know that too, I do, I do! What's the name of her daughter, Papa?'

Uri thought for a moment, the children's curiosity had somehow saved us all from breaking down. 'Princess Nefertiti,' he smiled.

'How long will you go away, Papa?' Tanya asked.

'Five years, my darling. You will be thirteen and Anna will be eleven, practically grown up, when I return.'

'Can't you stay with us? What will become of our mother?' Anna cried.

There were tears in Uri's eyes as he held his two little daughters even closer and I could see he was close to breaking down again. 'Mother Russia must come first, my darlings. She has decided I must go away.' Two tears rolled slowly down Uri's cheeks.

'Is she more important than our mother?' Tanya asked incredulously.

'She is the mother of everyone in Russia and cannot be denied,' I said, saving Uri from a reply which might upset his children. I felt that my heart should break and my lips trembled as I fought to hold back my tears.

Little Anna climbed from her father's knee and skipped from the room, apparently satisfied with the answer and not understanding the implications of Uri's departure. She returned a few minutes later with a small ginger kitten in her arms which she held up to her father. 'You must give it to Queen Cleopatra, Papa. It is a gift from all of us.'

Uri took the kitten, which practically disappeared in his big surgeon's hands. He was too overcome to protest or to disappoint his youngest daughter and so he put the kitten into the pocket of his great coat. 'Thank you, darling.' He kissed Anna and then Tanya. 'I shall ask Cleopatra's cat to let you know how things go for us in Egypt.'

'Cats can't write letters!' Anna exclaimed.

Uri patted the pocket of his overcoat. 'I will teach this one to write, just you see.'

At that moment the captain in charge of the

escorting militia entered the room. 'It is time to go, Surgeon Shebaldin,' he said.

When, perhaps two days later, I had stopped weeping continuously for my husband, I sat quietly thinking what might become of us. Uri had always been a loving and considerate husband and a wonderful father and the emotional burden of bringing up the two girls on my own seemed overwhelming. I tried to capture every moment of his last few hours with us, his strength and the reassurance that he would return, that five years was not so long. That we would leave Russia with the girls and go elsewhere and make a fresh start. It was then that I thought briefly of the kitten taken by Anna from a litter in the stables. I confess, I gave it scarcely a moment's thought, it was no more than a small detail in the tragedy of losing my husband forever. I simply assumed Uri would have given the kitten to someone as he was much too kind a man to simply leave it to die. Then, some weeks later, Anna came into breakfast one morning and asked why we hadn't yet received a letter from Cleopatra's cat?

'It has been five weeks. Is Egypt so far away that Papa hasn't arrived yet? Or do you think I gave him a stupid cat, Mama?'

Tanya sighed heavily. 'Egypt is a long way away, so they haven't even arrived yet,' she said firmly. 'Besides, you can't teach a cat to write in five weeks, silly!'

I thought for a moment that I should enlighten them, tell them the truth about their papa. But then I changed my mind, they were simply too young to face the prospect of never seeing their father again. There are, after all, many ways to handle one's personal grief and the notion of my beloved Uri arriving at the court of the Queen of Egypt on a diplomatic posting from the Tsar seemed no less improbable than the reason he was being sent to Siberia. So I confess I allowed myself to indulge a little in the children's fantasy.

'If anyone can teach a cat to write, it is your papa,' I said. 'I feel sure that we will soon have news from Cleopatra's cat, who will tell us how your darling papa is getting on.'

Anna was a persistent child and two months later she asked again why we hadn't heard from Cleopatra's cat. The cat was no longer a possessive noun in Anna's mind, she pronounced it as though the name of the cat was simply 'Cleopatra's Cat'.

I wrote every week to Uri, sending my letter to

an address he had given me, a hospital in a town in south-western Siberia nearest to where the salt mines are located. Russia, he argued, has few enough doctors and even fewer surgeons. Uri was confident that once he had arrived at his destination, the authorities would not throw away the services of a perfectly good surgeon, but would put him to work in the prison hospital. Or, if no such institution existed, then in the hospital of the town nearest to the prison camp.

However, it was a logical assumption in a country where logic and commonsense play a very minor part in the behaviour of the bureaucracy. It had been four and a half months since I had first written to him, and I had received no replies to my letters. My beloved Uri had simply disappeared from the face of the earth.

I was in a terrible dilemma about whether or not I should tell my children that their father had gone away and would never return. The notion that the cat would write had gathered momentum, and they had become obsessed with the need to hear from it.

Perhaps I, too, needed the comfort of knowing my husband was still alive. Hope, after all, is said to spring eternal, and I confess that my grief had left me in a state where I was incapable of making decisions which required strength of will. My two precious little daughters were all I had left in life and to cause them to share my misery, though it may in the long run have proved to be a wiser thing to do, was quite beyond me.

So I decided to write them letters from Cleopatra's Cat. I soon convinced myself that this was not as silly as it seemed. I would continue to write to Uri, but now the letters could be channelled through Cleopatra's Cat. I could reply to letters which it would seem we had received and the girls would then retain some sense of their beloved father, and he would remain a significant and loving influence in their young lives.

I will give you a small and, perhaps trite, example:

Tell Papa that we know he is too busy to write and on a secret mission for Mother Russia but that we love him and miss him. With all our love to him come lots of strokes for you,

Love Tanya, Anna and Sophia.

Tell him never a day passes when he isn't in our thoughts.

P.S. Your brothers and sisters in the stables are practically grown up and are almost capable of earning their living at catching mice of which there are a great many after the warmer winter. What are the Egyptian mice like, do they also have fleas? Anna wants to know. S, T & Little A.

I would write long letters to the children describing the land of Egypt and life in the royal palace of Cleopatra. There were stories of expeditions on the royal barge down the Nile, each full of adventures and excitement, all of which were seen from a cat's viewpoint, of course.

I told them that a cat in Egypt had almost the same status as a priest and that life was pretty cushy. That because I was the only ginger cat in Egypt I was considered to be the most beautiful cat in the whole world. My best friend, naturally, was Princess Nefertiti and I told them about the exotic life of a royal princess, and I included all the things I wanted my own little daughters to learn. I wrote that Nefertiti and I were inseparable and that Cleopatra even required me to be seated on her lap during royal occasions, and how I wore a collar of emeralds and rubies. The most special of these occasions was when the diplomatic corps were presented to the queen. I added that Papa was always the one singled out by Cleopatra. He was her absolutely favourite diplomat and confidant, greatly honoured because, of course, I was Russian and wondrously beautiful, and the two of us were bringing great honour to Mother Russia in Egyptian diplomatic circles.

The letters went on and on, telling of plots and conspiracies in the royal court and how I, Cleopatra's Cat, friend, seeker after the truth, brilliant spy, could travel silently and unseen over the rooftops. And under a starry midnight sky venture into the palaces of the foreign diplomats and hear of the plots and intrigues and the salacious gossip of the foreigners.

The important information I would, of course, take to Uri and the juicy bits of gossip directly to the queen herself. Increasingly, the queen came to depend on the Russian diplomat Uri Shebaldin to inform her of any danger to her throne while at the same time she revelled in the bedchamber gossip I supplied, often using it to taunt to the point of despair or to disconcert a pompous foreigner.

The two girls grew terribly anxious when several

of Cleopatra's Cat's letters related how diplomats from other countries began to bring the Queen of Egypt and her daughter Nefertiti cats as gifts. Siamese and Persian cats and Manx cats with no tails; Tibetan cats with brilliant blue eyes and Bengal felines that looked like tiny leopards. Cats of every description, temperament, colour and consistency of fur. Cats with almond eyes black as Mesopotamian olives, cats with pink noses, and some dark as midnight with sharply pointed ears and collars of South Sea pearls, all proffered in an attempt to win the queen's favour. But to no avail, Cleopatra's Cat won every contest with her agility, beauty and intelligence and remained the topmost cat in Egypt.

The adventures of Cleopatra's Cat and the Queen of Egypt grew more and more extravagant as I invented a new life for Uri, who through his knowledge of surgery had saved many an important Egyptian personage. I added that he was loved by the peasants who tilled the fields and sailed the graceful dhows on the Nile because he never spared himself and would operate on a camel driver or goat herd as readily as a prince or temple priest.

I even utilised the principal reason for our

tragedy and wrote a letter from Cleopatra's Cat telling how Uri had saved the life of Princess Nefertiti when she had burst her appendix. Naturally I invented a happy ending when Cleopatra's Cat told the girls how their father was showered with fresh honours by the queen, and was the envy of all the foreign countries for saving the life of the beautiful princess.

There was even a story of how the British Ambassador had swallowed a fish bone at a diplomatic dinner and was in danger of choking to death and how Uri had opened his throat on the spot with a meat skewer and removed the lethal bone. For this life-saving act a grateful British government had given him the title of *Sir Uri Shebaldin, Surgeon to the Queen of Egypt*. From that moment on each of the letters from Cleopatra's Cat ended with the words: *Another Cat-astrophe avoided by Sir Uri Shebaldin, Surgeon to the Queen of Egypt, the purr-fect physician!*

But little girls grow bigger every day and soon the five years Uri had promised them he would be away would be up. I had not received a word from my husband from the day of his departure. I had written to him every week enclosing both a copy of

Cleopatra's Cat's letter from Egypt and our reply, telling him of our little lives in St Petersburg and how we missed and loved him with all our hearts.

Now with the girls demanding their father's return I wrote a desperate letter from Cleopatra's Cat saying that so many Egyptian people had been saved from certain death by the miracle of Uri's surgery that Queen Cleopatra had begged Tsar Nicholas to let him stay a while longer. The cat wrote that she was personally bitterly disappointed by the Tsar's agreement that Uri could remain at the Court of Egypt to serve the interests of Mother Russia for a further two years.

I was playing for time, but, of course, the game was up. Tanya and Anna had put pressure on me precisely so that I would come clean. In fact, for some time they had been going along with the letters, having decided that it would please me to continue the fantasy long after they had suspected the truth. They understood that I needed to write the Cleopatra's Cat letters to maintain my own courage.

But as we say, '*Now* is as good as a poke with a stick.' We had just completed breakfast one morning when Tanya looked up and said, 'Mama, Papa isn't coming back, is he?'

Before I could reply Anna piped in. 'He's been sent to Siberia, hasn't he?'

While I had been expecting this moment, after all Tanya was nearly thirteen and Anna past her eleventh birthday, it nevertheless came as a shock. The letters from Cleopatra's Cat, albeit from my own pen, had become such an intrinsic part of our lives that I had somehow never given up the hope that Uri was still alive and would some day return to us. One morning we would look up at the sound of the doorbell and when we opened the door there he would be. A little thinner perhaps, with grey streaks in his hair, but that old familiar grin, his big surgeon's hands dangling at his sides, and perched on his shoulder would be a big ginger cat.

Now, confronted by my moment of truth, I looked out of the window onto the street, not knowing what to say to my two lovely daughters. Through my tears I could see the postman coming down the street and, not wishing to have Tanya and Anna see me crying, I said, 'Quick, both of you, there's the postman, run and see if there isn't a letter for us from Egypt.'

'Oh, Mama!' Tanya cried. 'I am so sorry to have hurt you!' But she went with Anna to the door and then outside to meet the postman. My eyes were filled with tears so I couldn't see them standing outside the window, nor even the postman as he handed them a letter. Tanya came back into the parlour followed by Anna and both stood silently by my side as I sobbed. Then Tanya pulled a chair out from the dining-room table and Anna took me by the hand. They guided me into the chair so that I sat with my elbows on the table and my face covered by my hands. I simply couldn't stop sobbing and I didn't quite know why. After all, I had always known this moment must come.

'Mama, there is a letter,' I heard Tanya saying, but it was as though her voice came to me in a fog. I then realised that she had been repeating this statement for some time. Then I felt her shaking my shoulder. 'Mama, there is a letter, I think from Siberia.'

Sophia Shebaldin glances up at us. 'I swear it on my mother's grave, the letter arrived the very morning, just like I said, the very morning the girls finally demanded to know about their father.'

Sophia Shebaldin looks as though she's about to stop the story right there, for she strokes the front of her dress.

'Please do not stop now!' Mr Mendelsohn begs. 'A letter from your husband? It is good news? He is coming back maybe, yes?'

Sophia Shebaldin smiles.

The letter was only a few words.

Make a great feast, Cleopatra's Cat is returning home. The letter is in the bottom of the cage.

What followed was a date and the time the Trans-Siberian train came into the grand station at St Petersburg.

It was such a tiny note, but it told us everything we needed to know. Uri had received my letters, he was alive and he was coming home. What was meant by the words *The letter is in the bottom of the cage* was impossible to tell. Though it didn't seem to matter now that we knew he was alive.

I grabbed the two girls and we danced and hugged and kissed and lay on the carpet, holding hands and giggling. It was the greatest day of our lives. 'A feast!' I said, jumping up. 'Invitations must be sent, cooks engaged, new uniforms made for the maids, spring cleaning to be done! We will call it the Feast of Cleopatra's Cat!' The girls both clapped their hands and laughed at this grand notion, after all it was Cleopatra's Cat who had saved us from despair and kept our hopes alive.

You can imagine the excitement when the train pulled in. I had bought a new outfit for each of us. Tanya and Anna both wore pale-blue taffeta dresses with grown-up mutton-leg sleeves, matching blue ribbons in their hair and the new single-strap English-style button across patent-leather shoes. I wore a chocolate-brown grosgrain costume that fitted tightly round the waist with a flare at the top of the hips, and a tapered skirt that boldly showed a snatch of ankle above red shoes with an outrageously high six-centimetre heel, the latest in Paris fashion. All of this was set off by a beautiful hat decorated with scarlet and blue French ribbon and a peacock feather that seemed to brush the summer sky.

We looked frantically for Uri, not knowing what to expect. Would he be thin as a rake, aged, with his hair prematurely white, and perhaps even dressed in rags? Would he be using a walking stick? But I didn't care how he came back to us, I simply wanted his big surgeon's hands to be wrapped around me, our little family together again.

But soon the platform was empty, the other passengers had all left and the porters had taken their barrows piled high with bags so that only the two girls and myself were left standing on the platform. The engine hissed intermittently, its *shhhh* of steam not subtracting, but somehow adding to the silence and the desolation of the empty train platform.

Then an official in a smart uniform and cap stepped off the train carrying a clipboard. He looked up briefly in our direction and then commenced to walk purposefully towards us. 'Mrs Shebaldin?'

I nodded.

'Follow me, please.' Without a further word of explanation he turned and walked towards the furthest end of the train.

Of course! I suddenly thought. Uri is ill, why didn't I think of that! Relief flooded through me.

'What is it, Mama?' Tanya asked, sensing my anxiety and then my sudden relief. Anna grabbed my hand, saying nothing, suddenly she was a little girl again.

'I don't know, darling,' I replied. 'Perhaps your papa is not well?'

We stopped at last at the very end carriage. It was different to the other carriages and was without windows, but with ventilation slits that sat high up on its blank sides. The official produced a set of keys and unlocked the carriage door. It was a heavy door and he had to force it open with his shoulder.

'He is in there, madam.' He pointed into the dark interior of the carriage and then turned and looked down the platform. 'Have you not made arrangements to have him removed?' Then he shrugged and pushed the clipboard under my nose. 'Sign here, please. There are two items, a sealed lead coffin and one live cat in a large bird cage.'

Slow tears run down Sophia Shebaldin's face and I see that Anya and Tamara are both weeping softly and that Mr Mendelsohn is also sniffing. I must admit a big lump is also sitting in my throat and I can barely see the frying pan bubbling away on the fire.

'There was a letter in a false bottom of Cleopatra's Cat's cage,' Sophia says slowly. 'A wonderful long letter, it was from a fellow prisoner and I have it here with me.'

She reaches into the bodice of her dress and brings out a small linen bag. Her long, hard fingers

work at the knot which ties the end and Sophia
Shebaldin removes the letter. There is a full moon
that night and now she looks up, the light from the
moon softening her small, sharp features. Then she
begins to read.

Dear Madam Shebaldin,

*I am writing to you as a friend and great admirer
of the late and truly great surgeon Uri Shebaldin.
Or should I say Sir Uri Shebaldin, Surgeon to the
Queen of Egypt? Uri died this morning in the company of five thousand men who loved him and will
mourn him every day that remains of their short
and precarious lives.*

*Allow me to explain, madam. Life in a Gulag is
measured by the extent to which a man will struggle
to survive, whether that is at the expense of another
is of no importance. Feeling and compassion are
luxuries reserved for those who are free, here survival is the only purpose and a measure of a man's
worth. How to stay alive is the singular thought and
destroys any concept of decency or morality. A man
who would think otherwise would not last a month in
this place. That is, any other man but your husband.*

I was in the cattle truck with him when he first

produced the tiny ginger kitten from his pocket and held it up. There was, I recall, a great deal of laughter at the tiny creature held aloft and one of the prisoners shouted, 'It is not even sufficient for a poor man's breakfast!' Uri laughed along with all of us, but then he said, 'If it survives, comrades, then we all survive! This cat will be our talisman! A cat has nine lives and we are going to need every one of them if we are ever to return from Siberia to our homes!'

Men are superstitious creatures and from that moment the little ginger kitten became very important to all of us. Somehow we kept it alive on the long journey to Siberia and when we arrived at the Gulag we took turns to protect the kitten from becoming a tasty morsel for a starving prisoner who was not in our group.

Starvation here in the slave camps is one's only constant companion. A small slice of black bread and a dish of hot water with perhaps a rotten slice of carrot and a lump of potato no bigger than your thumb is all we get from the authorities, the rest we must find for ourselves. We all carry a small forage tin on our belts and as we work we look for things to eat, a few fat grubs under a piece of bark or some *small plant root, or edible leaf. Sometimes, if we are lucky, a wild mushroom, though very little grows here in the tundra.*

When it rains, things are better, this is the time when the earthworms come to the surface and a man can gather a dozen or more in his tin if he is lucky. They are very good to eat. (To a starving man, any protein is a gift from God!) But, no matter how hungry we were, if our cat passed by, any of us would give her a share of our worms. Cleopatra's Cat was not only loved but also most useful. In the dry weather she could locate where there were worms under the soil and many a man was saved from starvation by her remarkable nose. When she killed a rat we would give her the head and the tail and the rest would go into the pot. Any prisoner supposing he would turn the cat into a meal would himself have been instantly killed.

Cleopatra's Cat became the sign to us that survival in the salt mines was possible, and that we would someday go home again. But it was not only the cat that kept our hopes up, it was also the letters the cat wrote and your replies. They were smuggled in from the hospital and, after Surgeon Shebaldin had read them, they were passed from hand to hand and read aloud to those who could not read. Your little family became at once all our families and we took to thinking of ourselves as 'the Egyptians' and you gave us something to hope for.

You see, madam, Uri Shebaldin was everything Cleopatra's Cat said he was in her letters from Egypt. He was a diplomat with the authorities, often saving a prisoner from a terrible beating or even death at the hands of a guard or camp official. Moreover, his scalpel worked ceaselessly in the little cottage hospital.

For instance, on the very first night we arrived, he saved the life of the son of the camp commandant by removing a brain tumour. In the past five years his remarkable surgeon's hands have saved hundreds of lives.

Sir Uri Shebaldin, Surgeon to the Queen of Egypt, has performed some of the most remarkable new operations in Russia and all in the small, inadequate hospital in the nearby town. I am forbidden to give you its name though I know you know it because of the letters.

For the sake of his colleagues at the Academy of Medicine in St Petersburg I shall enumerate some of these medical breakthroughs. I too am a doctor, but of a much lower order, a medic, a pill pusher, no more. Uri's post-operative notes are included with this letter for the benefit of students and teachers at the academy. He developed techniques for removing gastric and duodenal ulcers and performed what he termed gastroenterostomies (notes attached). With a high degree of success, he removed cancers from the large bowel and the rectum and developed a method whereby he operated on cancer of the rectum through the area between the anus and the genitals.

You must excuse my language, Madam Shebaldin, but you are a medical family and I know will take no exception to this terminology. Finally, Uri Shebaldin became the absolute master of the appendicectomy, saving countless lives with this one operative procedure alone.

Uri died after a typhoid epidemic in the slave camps, where he worked incessantly to save others' lives. His dying wish was that we should try to return Cleopatra's Cat to little Anna and Tanya, and that you should know the good you have brought to thousands of condemned men. But for your letters they would have thought their lives hopeless and died long before completing their sentences. Despair is the true epidemic of Siberia. Now many believe they will return to their homes, and some already have.

I must confess that several of the men asked that you not be told of your husband's death as they have become addicted to the letters from Egypt. But decency and a love of Surgeon Shebaldin prevailed, not a simple occurrence in a place where both these commodities are almost unknown. Your husband asked as his dying wish that, if Cleopatra's Cat should come home, you hold a great feast for her and, at the same time, light a candle in his memory. He also fervently desires that you should marry again and be happy.

We have persuaded the authorities to return his body to you, though it is sealed in lead and may not be opened for fear that the typhoid may spread. You must honour your husband by complying strictly with this request. Besides, he would wish you to remember him as he was when he left his beloved family.

My own sentence has five years yet to run and I do not suppose I shall leave this place alive. May God bless you and your children. It remains only for me to say that my life has been made richer by the gifts of your husband whom I counted as my friend. Cleopatra's Cat is now returned to you and I hope will survive a difficult journey accompanying the body of Sir Uri Shebaldin, Surgeon to the Queen of Egypt.

My salutations to your two lovely daughters. I remain, madam, your faithful admirer,

Alexander Proknikoff, Medical Doctor.

What a feast was prepared, and Cleopatra's Cat was the centre of attention as students and teachers from the Academy of Medicine and all our friends celebrated his death in true Russian style. Uri's notes were welcomed at the academy and he was hailed as a true hero of Mother Russia. A year later the Tsar presented me with the Medal of Honour, Second Class, and a military band played at the ceremony in the great square outside the Winter Palace. At the presentation the principal of the academy spoke of Uri as a remarkable surgeon and announced that a new and modern operating theatre would be built in his honour and named after him.

. . .

Sophia Shebaldin gives a brief smile. 'My beloved husband had been completely exonerated as well as vindicated and now Mother Russia clasped our little family to her fond bosom. The so-called Bolshevik surgeon was the hero of the hour and those who had maliciously brought about his downfall and his death now hurried to kiss my hand.'

Sophia Shebaldin shrugs. 'I thank you for your patience and for taking me into your small group. I feel humble that you would welcome me.' She pauses and smiles, looking at each of us. 'And that, my dear friends, is the end of my little story.'

We all clap furiously, it is a wonderful tale and, despite the interruptions, very well told. Of course, the one question on all of our minds is how, with all the honours and posthumous fame bestowed on Uri Shebaldin, Sophia Shebaldin should come to be in our little group, which is definitely no place for the rich or famous. But I am glad to say that we hold our tongues. Even Olga Zorbatov manages to remain *stumm*.

That night we eat with relish. After all, it is not every night we are privileged to hear a good story and, at the same time, enjoy a truly delicious horsemeat stew to match it. When we finish eating, to our surprise and, I must say, delight, Sophia Shebaldin offers to tell us the remainder of her remarkable adventure.

'I wanted that you should eat in a happy frame of mind,' she explains. 'It was a lovely dinner tonight, Mrs Moses, and I didn't want to spoil it with talk of sorrow.' She pauses. 'I thank you for your good manners, for not demanding to know how I have come to be with all of you on the road to freedom.'

We all grin rather sheepishly, she had guessed at our curiosity and disappointment and now she was rewarding us.

'The great flu epidemic of 1907 took Tanya and little Anna,' Sophia Shebaldin says quietly and then she begins to weep softly. I put my arm around her, but she gently shakes me away. 'I am such a coward,' she sobs, 'but I can bear it no longer. Mother Russia has destroyed us completely, there is no more happiness for me in this old, cruel land.'

She sniffs and wipes her tears on the sleeve of her dress, then sniffs again and lifts her chin defiantly. 'I shall go to London where I will search for a ginger cat. Then, together, we will take the boat to Egypt where I will sit on the edge of the desert and dream and my English cat will nap in the sun.' Sophia Shebaldin seems to be thinking for a moment, then adds, 'I shall put up a sign outside my little home which reads "Foot Doctor". There will always be people passing by who suffer from sore and weary feet. I shall restore them and send them on their way.' She smiles brightly, 'So, you see, we will always have sufficient to eat.' She then adds, as though it is necessary to justify this notion of going to Egypt, 'An old woman and a ginger cat, whom I shall name Sir Frederick Treves, do not require much to stay alive.' She looks up and although the night is warm she appears to shiver. 'My bones are so very cold, I go to warm them in the desert sunlight and to rest at night under an Arabian sky pricked by a million stars.'

There is silence and then, to my surprise, Mr Petrov speaks. 'And what happened to Cleopatra's Cat, Madam Shebaldin?'

Sophia Shebaldin laughs, a genuine laugh that comes from her stomach, one we have never heard before. It is pretty and light-hearted and makes us all feel good. Then she spreads her arms wide with her palms open and upwards. 'You know cats, Mr Petrov. They don't like to be moved. Cleopatra's Cat was last seen catching the train back to Siberia. If you ask me, another *cat*-astrophe in the making!'

TO THE

FOUR

WINDS

Here I take up the author's voice again, for although Mrs Moses told me most of what happened to the characters in her sojourn, some details concerning the whereabouts of people was gathered from letters to her which she left in my care. Still other information came to me through my own research efforts.

Mrs Moses's group eventually crossed into Poland where the Polish authorities, sick and tired of people fleeing from Russia, put them into a cattle truck and moved them to the German border.

Mrs Moses and her little group were most grateful for the lift across Poland, a country they collectively regarded as being very little improvement on Russia. In Germany they noticed that a lot of marching was going on and that there seemed to be soldiers everywhere. Mrs Moses had had enough of soldiers, whom she saw as the same old hunters, whatever their uniform.

She appealed to a Jewish refugee agency, which provided them with train tickets and food to get them to Paris. It was only when they arrived in Paris that they finally broke up and went their separate ways . . .

THE TWELVE LOST TRIBES
OF CALIFORNIA

Firstly there were the children in the group, all of them orphans except for little Tanya, Anya's child, who had survived the Cossack attack in the arms of Mrs Moses. Belonging to no one, the children had simply joined the journey along the way, they couldn't recall ever having belonged to a family other than perhaps a ragamuffin gang living on the streets of some faraway town or city. Left alone, most of them would almost certainly have come to a sad ending, preyed upon by the evil elements in every society, to become thieves, drunkards and prostitutes.

The great trek out of the Russian wilderness under the leadership and love of Mrs Moses was the first time they had experienced affection of any kind. Although Olga Zorbatov was a real pain in the *toukis* (the bum) to all the adults, the kids loved her even more than they loved Anya, which is saying a whole heap.

With twelve children to feed, Olga Zorbatov eventually got to California and then to the city of Los Angeles. Her husband Sergei was still sending her nightly messages from the stars, and she set up as a psychic.

Her timing was perfect. Nestled among the orange orchards in the tiny hamlet of Hollywood, the fledgling Californian movie industry was just beginning to stir. The silent movies needed kids and Olga Zorbatov had twelve hungry mouths to feed. Her dozen little ragamuffins, who worked as a perfect team, were a movie director's dream. They could and would do anything for a laugh and seemed to have no fear. Maybe you've seen some of those very old silent movies on TV? For instance, the kids in Max Sennett's first Hollywood movies were mostly Mrs Z's orphans or what she referred to as 'One each of the Lost Tribes of Israel plus One.'

Mrs Z had given the children all the same

surname, though not her own. When she had landed at Ellis Island in New York the clerk had asked her for her name. 'These are your children, Mrs Zorbatov?' the official asked, then, 'Give me their names please.'

'Moses, all are Moses!' Mrs Z declared.

The immigration officer was accustomed to confusion and he sighed, it was going to be a long day. 'All are called Moses Zorbatov?'

Olga Zorbatov was losing patience with the stupid man. 'No, me I am Zorbatov, they Moses,' she grabbed a small girl, 'Tanya Moses!' Then she pointed to a boy, 'Ivan Moses!'

The official nodded his head. 'And where is Mrs Moses?' he asked.

'She go to Australia,' Olga declared.

'Well, with twelve children I can't say I blame her?' the weary immigration officer answered, then began the task of writing down the names of the children and appending Moses to each of them.

Olga Zorbatov had named all the children in honour of Mrs Moses who she said had led them all out of the wilderness. Because there were twelve children, she likened it to Moses leading the tribes of Israel out of bondage. She was not a Jew herself, nor, for that matter, did she suppose any of the children were, that is but for one small boy named Moshe who was circumcised and so became her Plus One. She told them that each of them came from one of the eleven lost tribes of Israel, while Moshe with the missing foreskin was *kosher*, that is to say, he came from the Hebrew tribe, the one that didn't manage to get itself lost.

With her fortune-telling and her children playing crowd scenes and bit parts and running messages on the film lots she managed to survive, and she boasted that her lost tribes had never gone without a meal in America.

Then, one day, she hit upon her one really big idea. She decided to open the first casting agency in Hollywood.

Actually, it wasn't her idea, and in truth, she never claimed it was, giving all the credit instead to her husband from whom she still took her instructions as he *schlepped* across the midnight sky, riding on the tail of this or that sign of the zodiac. She named her casting agency 'Casting to the Stars', not because the word 'Star' had any meaning in the movie industry at that time, but because her beloved husband, that is Sergei Zorbatov,

Grand Chef and Professor of Astrological Science and Zodiac Law, instructed that she should name it after the star-studded firmament. He had always claimed that heaven was the great kitchen of human possibilities. Mrs Z maintained that it was Sergei's naming of her agency that was the major element in its success.

So successful was Mrs Z at picking acting talent that the very word 'Star' as a description for actors who made the big time is derived from the name of Olga Zorbatov's casting agency. It survives to this day, though under a different name. Apparently she had neglected to register the name and so the term 'Casting to the Stars' was pinched by the proliferation of casting consultancies that emerged over the years, so that as a term it has become almost a cliché. When this happened Mrs Z changed the name of her agency to Central Casting of Hollywood.

As for what happened to each of the eleven Lost Tribes of Israel Plus One, that is another story and another book. But then a great many books have been written about the great American dream and the world doesn't need another one.

Olga Zorbatov never married ('Sergei would kill me!') and she eventually died at the comparatively young age of sixty. Her funeral was attended by ten of her lost tribes, including her Plus One, Moshe, together with thirty-nine of her grandchildren and one hundred and three great-grandchildren.

In her last will and testament Olga Zorbatov didn't bequeath a cent to any of them, instead leaving nearly eight million dollars to establish a Chair of Astrological Science at the University of California. It is no coincidence that California has been producing highly intelligent nutcases and weirdos ever since.

THE CHICKENS WHO
LOVED TCHAIKOVSKY

Of Anya and Mr Mendelsohn a quieter story. They too went to America, straight to Boston where Mr Mendelsohn was disappointed to find that the famous symphony orchestra was not for sale, not even for all the pearls in the South Sea.

However, he did eventually become its First Violin. He married Anya in the Russian Orthodox Church in Boston, which was what she wanted. In return she gave him two more sons and made him chicken and mushroom soup every night of his life.

Alas, the soup was not as good as her Russian concoctions, which concerned her greatly, and she often lamented that she was unable to find the various types of mushrooms she required. She also complained about the chickens. 'American chickens eat the wrong kind of worms,' she'd say. 'Maybe making a living for worms is too easy in America and they don't work hard enough to give the chicken meat the best flavour. Also, there is no blue corn to feed them.'

Later in her life, when battery hens came into vogue, she got really angry and cashed in the last of the mermaid's pearls and started her own chicken farm.

When Mr Mendelsohn eventually retired from the Boston Symphony Orchestra he would play to the chickens morning and night. 'It's not maybe so glamorous as mermaids,' he would say, 'but, believe me, a chicken has better taste in music.' In fact, Anya's chickens loved his whole repertoire and in particular Tchaikovsky. This especially endeared them to him and they returned the compliment by laying the best eggs in America.

Anya imported worms and mushroom spawn from Russia and a sack of best blue corn which she sowed by hand in the traditional peasant manner. The worms thrived in her compost heap, the mushrooms flourished in a disused horse stable and the corn took to the more democratic American climate which resulted in one bumper crop after another. Soon Mr Mendelsohn was enjoying chicken soup second to none, the best in the world, whatever country you care to name in chicken-soup competition, including Israel.

Their three children grew to adulthood, the daughter born with Mrs Moses on the road in Russia and the two sons in America, and together they opened a restaurant called Mr Mendelsohn's Chicken Spit, which sold barbecue chicken and chicken and mushroom soup (six varieties of mushroom skilfully blended). Later, as they began to expand, they adapted the name of their several restaurants to Mr Chicken Spit, a chain which boasted that it used only free-range chickens and White Russian field mushrooms (the Cold War was still on). Today it is called The Chicken Spit and is a franchise operation which has eight hundred outlets in America and another six hundred throughout the world. Next year the first Chicken Spit opens in Red Square in Moscow directly opposite Lenin's tomb. Anya's grandchild, Michael Mendelsohn, who graduated *summa cum laude* at MIT with a Master of Science in Food Technology, is now chief executive of CSI Inc. (Chicken Spit International) and will be there with the Foreign Secretary, who will officially open the first Russian franchise.

It's a great pity that Anya and Mr Mendelsohn never lived to see this triumphant return to Mother Russia, though, admittedly, he would have been one hundred and eleven years old and she one hundred and sixteen.

Mr Mendelsohn died of a heart attack in 1961 while listening to Tchaikovsky's Symphony No. 4 on the radio and when Anya found him in his old leather armchair he still had a smile on his face.

That night Anya made chicken and mushroom soup as usual and then sat quietly beside Mr Mendelsohn, whom she had bathed and dressed in his best silk pyjamas and put into the bed they had shared for nearly fifty years. She sat beside him with the steaming bowl on a tray on her lap. 'I loved you, Mr Mermaid Man,' she said quietly, 'every day of our wonderful life.' The next morning she was found dead, still seated beside her beloved violinist, his beautiful hands with the long, elegant fingers clasped in her lap.

At the autopsy, traces of *Entoloma sinuatum* were discovered in Anya's stomach. It is also known as the Poison Chalice and is another of the clever little mushrooms a peasant girl from a Russian village makes it her business to know all about in case someday it comes in useful.

A HERO OF LENINGRAD

And now news of Tamara Polyansky, who also went to America where she joined the great Barnum & Bailey Circus as one of its leading attractions.

But not all migrant stories turn out happily ever after, and while she enjoyed great notoriety and top billing in the famous circus, Tamara was never really happy in America. She found it difficult to understand the American people who, on the surface, acted so friendly and after five minutes of acquaintance invited you into their homes, but seemed reluctant to enter into any deep or meaningful relationship. 'America,' she would say, 'is a mile wide and an inch deep, Russia is an inch wide and a mile deep. That is why we can never understand each other.'

On the surface she seemed to have everything, fame and fortune as well as beauty. But what Tamara Polyansky craved more than anything was love, to find another Eugene Wilenski, to fly with him through the air high above the gasping crowd and then later to hold him in her adoring arms while they made wonderful love.

What is perhaps the strangest thing of all is that she longed for Siberia where she had spent the first years of her circus life. Circus life is frantic and often quarrelsome, full of petty jealousy and backstabbing, where each performer competes with the others for a higher billing position on the circus posters or a bigger name in lights outside the big top. Moreover, circuses in America were often attached to country fairs, rodeos, Fourth of July parades and all the razzamatazz of an immature people, and Tamara, increasingly, longed for the quiet of the endless tundra and the deep respect Russians hold for a great artist.

Tamara Polyansky's desire for solitude was probably some sort of romantic notion brought about by too much suffering and tragedy in her life.

The Russian personality is very big on suffering and the American not at all keen on it, so Tamara may have come to believe that what she now craved was the solitude of Siberia, having entirely forgotten how awful it had been in the first place.

Tamara tried to leave the circus when she met and married a dashing young American flyer, five years younger than herself. Not a trapeze flyer, but a young airman who flew a Sopwith Camel in the United States Air Corps. But again her timing was lousy and tragedy struck once more when her young husband was shot down and killed over France in 1917 on the first day the Americans saw combat in the air during the Great War.

He was shot down by an Australian infantry soldier who, not recognising the insignia painted on the wings of the biplane, thought it must belong to the enemy. By some incredible fluke he hit Tamara's airman between the eyes with a single bullet from his Lee Enfield rifle. He got reprimanded and Tamara got the usual 'Killed in Action' telegram from Washington.

'Must all the men in my life be shot down!' was all she said when she got the telegram. Then, dry-eyed, she packed her bags.

With the death of her American airman and with the advent of the Russian Revolution that year, Tamara remembered the parting words of Count Tolstoy as he lay dying in the little railway station shed. *Child, leave Russia and return only when the Tsar and those like him have been overthrown.* Miss Showbiz decided to take the advice of the world's greatest writer and she returned to Moscow.

For many years after her return she and Mrs Moses exchanged letters and it seemed that Tamara was happy enough. The communists, anxious to stamp their mark on the proletariat, made her a professor at the Academy of Circus and Ballet in Moscow, where she taught acrobatics, the highwire and trapeze and so became a founding member of the now world-famous Moscow Circus. For her brilliant work she was made a Hero of the Soviet Union and, surprisingly, just before the Second World War she was also made a colonel in the Soviet military forces and posted to a circus-training school in Leningrad to help train an entertainment battalion for the Red Army.

The last letter Mrs Moses received from Tamara Polyansky was in April 1941, and two months later the Germans invaded the USSR. It took Hitler only two and a half months to reach the outskirts of Leningrad, which, as the birthplace of Bolshevism, he swore to wipe from the face of the earth.

German troops commenced the siege of Leningrad on the 8th of September 1941 and continued until the 27th of January 1944. In Russian history, this great siege where ordinary people resisted the might of the greatest invasion in Russian history is simply called Nine Hundred Days.

By the time the Germans withdrew from Leningrad, utterly defeated and demoralised, a million ordinary Russian people and soldiers had perished defending the city. Many died from the ceaseless shelling but as many or more dropped dead of hunger and cold in the streets. And when no dogs, cats or rats were left to eat they ate the glue off the back of wallpaper. Mrs Moses prayed to God for every one of those nine hundred days and asked that He should spare her beloved Miss Showbiz.

In 1950 Mrs Moses received a letter and a small package from the Russian Department of War Veterans to say that Colonel Tamara Polyansky had died in the Siege of Leningrad defending her country. They had found her last will and testament which had been lodged before her posting to Leningrad, as was required with the Department of the Soviet Army in Moscow. She had left all her worldly possessions to Mrs Moses, 107 Campbell Parade, Bondi Beach, Sydney, Australia. The letter went on to say that her body had never been found and that there were no worldly possessions to inherit, but that to honour Colonel Polyansky's name the USSR enclosed for Mrs Moses the Medal of Hero of the Soviet Union, an inheritance more valuable to a Russian than life itself.

Poor Miss Showbiz. I hope she had some happy years jammed in somewhere between all the tragedy in her life. When Mrs Moses died she was buried with the medal awarded to Colonel Tamara Polyansky pinned to her chest. She said she would personally return it to its rightful owner when she got to heaven.

THE PROFESSOR AND
WHACKER'S SULPHUR-
CRESTED COCKATOO

The professor's story is somewhat different from the rest of Mrs Moses's little flock. He elected to go to England and when he was asked why he would choose it over America or one of the newer countries like Australia or New Zealand or even South Africa he shrugged. 'We have Shakespeare in common with the English, that is not a bad start.'

'Shakespeare? What has Russia got to do with Shakespeare? Tolstoy, who is practically still living, yes, but the Englishman is long dead and probably he never even came to Russia,' Mrs Moses said.

'Russian is the only language in which the

works of Shakespeare translate perfectly,' the professor said. 'That is enough for me, our hearts and our minds beat to the same rhythm, our tongues to the same cadence, I shall go to England, the English are the only civilised Russians!'

And that was that. Sometimes after hearing the professor carrying on, Mrs Moses took the trouble to thank the Lord that she wasn't clever.

However, it seems the professor must have known something because before you could say 'Stratford on Avon', he had been accepted at Oxford University as a don and lecturer in the Department of Russian Literature. And, it seems, he soon became famous, not so much for his lectures on Tolstoy, Dostoyevsky and Pushkin but for his bird-watching.

The English are notorious bird-watchers, or 'twitchers' as they are commonly called, and it seems that English academics and intellectuals are particularly keen on putting on their wellies and wading into marshes, getting cold, wet, hungry and devoured by insects or climbing into trees or hides until their bones ache with fatigue, simply to see the first robin in spring or the last swallow in autumn. The professor was soon upgraded to professorial status again, not because his insights into the works of Aleksandr Sergeyevich Pushkin or Fyodor Mikhailovich Dostoyevsky were all that remarkable, but because he seemed to know more about birds than anyone else at the world-famous university. Knowledge of such high order could not be invested in a lowly don and so he was immediately elevated to the rank of Professor.

Under the patronage of the collective twitchers of England who bought his books on exotic species of birds by the tens of thousands and attended his lectures to the Gould and Audubon Societies, the professor grew even more puffed up and pompous. Soon he was as stuffy and incomprehensible as all the other academics at Oxford, at which stage the English decided he was as close to being an Englishman as he was ever to get and that it was time to grant him full citizenship. He accepted in the name of Russia and of Shakespeare.

'The English are really Russians in disguise!' he was fond of saying. 'Shakespeare would have made an excellent Russian, make no mistakeski!'

The professor also corresponded with Mrs Moses in Australia although his letters tended to be long and complex and, for the most part, contained questions about parrots, galahs, budgerigars and cockatoos. Mrs Moses took his letters down to the Bondi Pet Shop and asked Whacker O'Sullivan, its owner, for the information the professor required.

Whacker would then scratch his head. 'Never thought a flamin' budgie was that complicated, Mrs Mo,' he'd say and then he'd volunteer to ask a bloke at the Australian Museum who drank at the same pub as him. The man from the museum usually knew the answers and Whacker, who couldn't remember his own name after a few beers, made the man from the museum write the information on the back of an empty cigarette pack.

When Mrs Moses came into the shop the next day he'd take a roll-yer-own he'd pre-rolled out of the empty cigarette pack and, in a normal, casual sort of voice which disguised the fact that he was reading, told her what the cove from the museum had written down.

After a few years, with Mrs Moses telling everyone about his expertise and with the professor himself mentioning his name as an authority on the parrots of the Antipodes in one of his famous bird books sent to Mrs Moses, Whacker O'Sullivan was considered to be a leading Australian expert on the genus.

That is, until the expert from the museum died of cirrhosis of the liver and Whacker was forced into having amnesia, brought about, he insisted, by a punch in the head sustained in a pub brawl. 'Me bird brain's gorn, Mrs Mo, can't remember a flamin' thing about them cockies no more.'

But at about the time Whacker O'Sullivan's bird brain was irrevocably destroyed, the professor's letters began to change. The Bolsheviks had taken over Russia in the 1917 Revolution and the Tsar and his family were murdered by the Reds, although their bodies hadn't been discovered.

The effect on the professor was profound. He loved the Princess Tatiana like his own daughter and he took the news of her death very badly. He seemed to lose all interest in life and his morbid letters dwelling on the demise of the princess soon precluded any mention of parrots, cockatoos, parakeets, galahs or budgerigars. The feathers had been completely ripped out of the professor as he mourned for his lovely princess who could imitate all the bird calls in the world.

After a while the professor's letters took what seemed, at first, a turn for the better. He'd convinced himself, because the Russian royal family had not been found, that the Reds hadn't killed them. And that they had been allowed to escape under the one condition that they never revealed their true identity to the outside world.

Mrs Moses hoped that the professor would let it rest at that and resume his interest in birds. But this was clearly not to be the case, as a letter followed which told her that the professor had decided to dedicate the rest of his life to flushing out the Russian royals.

Mrs Moses, reading between the lines, realised that the professor, who had always been a bit, you know, squiffy, had finally gone over the top and, to use her own expression, was now plain *meshuga*. So when Whacker O'Sullivan, who had kind of gotten used to feeling important when Mrs Moses brought the professor's letters into the pet shop with her parrot questions, asked why he hadn't written in quite a while, Mrs Moses confided that she was worried about her dear friend.

Whacker, always a notorious stickybeak, badgered her for more information.

Eventually Mrs Moses broke down and tearfully told Whacker how the professor had become obsessed with the notion that the Tsar and his family had escaped and were living incognito somewhere out of Russia. She pointed out in her somewhat broken English that this was a highly unlikely theory as you couldn't go around hiding an entire Russian royal family without someone eventually cottoning on.

Whacker thought about this for a while and then naturally he took the conundrum down to the pub with him. The way he told the story to the blokes in the pub, the Russian royal family had escaped the Reds but were all suffering from amnesia and were last seen boarding the boat in Southampton bound for Australia.

'Crikey, we could have flamin' royalty walking along Bondi Beach not knowing who the blazes they are!' was how he ended his sad tale.

While most of the drinkers thought this an unlikely story there were some who, while not being exactly intellectually challenged, were definitely on the stupid side. After a few more beers the rumour that the Russian royal family had been seen on Bondi Beach was taken home by every drunk with an Irish name in the pub, which meant practically everyone present after eight o'clock that night.

By morning Bondi Beach was awash with the rumour and by noon everyone was looking at anyone they didn't recognise as a local to see if he or she looked as though they might be a Russian. Not that anyone knew what a Russian was supposed to look like. 'Sort of foreign-looking with heavy eyebrows and women with long plaits and dark eyes but who you can see aren't, you know, your proper wogs. Oh yes, and wearing high boots with the bottoms of their pants tucked in.'

Fortunately it was winter and there were only a few people on the beach. But by four o'clock that afternoon an Italian with dark, heavy eyebrows from Leichhardt, a near inner-city suburb, together with his wife and five children had been spotted paddling on the beach. There was also a pair of suspicious-looking knee-high boots on the sand nearby and the man had his pants rolled up to his knees. This was evidence enough and the Russian royal family was promptly rounded up by a big crowd of locals, who escorted the loudly protesting and gesticulating husband and wife and their five tearful children to the local police station.

Whereupon Whacker O'Sullivan, stepping from the crowd, announced to Sergeant Bumper O'Flynn that the Ruski royals had been found wandering aimlessly along the beach, and that it was obvious they were suffering from amnesia and it was his civic duty to turn them in to the authorities.

When Bumper O'Flynn looked a trifle doubtful, Whacker duly pointed out that he was an expert in memory loss and so should recognise the condition when he came across it. 'Besides, can't you hear them, they're bloody speaking Russian, aren't they, mate?'

'Sounds more like Eye-talian,' the police sergeant suggested.

'Nah! It's fair dinkum Russian orright, London to a bloody brick, mate!' Whacker insisted.

As the Italian and his wife had not long arrived in Australia and couldn't yet speak English, they were yabbering away in a Sicilian dialect, which naturally enough everyone now took to be Russian. As nobody could understand Russian, Mrs Moses was immediately sent for.

In her traditional no-nonsense manner she soon got things sorted out and afterwards she got really cranky with Whacker O'Sullivan for creating such a ridiculous incident which, she claimed, brought shame on all the Russians in Bondi

Beach, who were, of course, as far as anyone knew, only herself.

Whacker, at heart a gentleman, was truly contrite and, in an effort to mollify Mrs Moses, offered to give the professor a sulphur-crested cockatoo, which he said would be delivered by a mate of his who was the second engineer on the *Duke of York*, a passenger steamer that sailed between England and Australia.

Mrs Moses was much taken by this idea. With such a handsome bird as his companion, the professor might snap out of his morbid preoccupation with the death of Princess Tatiana. The cocky was duly delivered by Whacker's engineer mate and a happy ending was hoped for by all.

But it was not to be. The professor's obsession grew worse. He had convinced himself that the Russian royal family had escaped and were living with their second cousin King George in Buckingham Palace as poor relations. Furthermore, that they were being kept in captivity against their will.

Before he went completely crazy he wrote to Mrs Moses to say that the lovely white cockatoo with the brilliant yellow plumage was a most excellent friend and that it personally and continually strengthened his resolve to find the missing Russian royals and to expose the King of England. This was probably because Whacker, who was still far from convinced that the professor's theory wasn't correct, hadn't told Mrs Moses that he'd taught the cocky to say, 'The princess lives! The princess lives!'

The ending is maybe sad and maybe not, it all depends on how you look at life. The professor, by now impoverished, spent the remainder of his days outside Buckingham Palace with a sandwich board draped over his ancient great coat. Painted on the board were the words: *Free Russia's royal family – The Tsar is a bird-watcher!*

Never separated from the professor was the beautiful Australian sulphur-crested cockatoo, who sat on his shoulder squawking, 'The princess lives! The princess lives!' What's more, every day, winter and summer, all the birds of England, the robins, wrens, thrushes, larks, sparrows and the rest of the birds of the air would come and visit, pecking at the breadcrumbs the professor would habitually rub into his beard. People would stop and watch in wonder and most would leave a coin in the old felt hat which lay at the professor's feet. In fact, so popular a tourist attraction did the old man become that the hat filled with coins several times a day and the professor was forced to take a taxi to Barclay's Bank every evening and then home to where he lived under Chelsea Bridge.

When Professor Ivan Mikhaylovich Slotinowitz died in 1938 he received a splendid obituary in *The Times* of London. The obit mentioned in passing that he had left a bequest of ten thousand pounds towards building an aviary at the London Zoo.

What with the Second World War and things, the bequest was sort of forgotten and it was more than twenty years later, with the interest on the original capital having accumulated, that the great aviary was commissioned by the custodians of London Zoo to be designed by Lord Snowdon. This, the professor would have liked a lot, Lord Snowdon having once been married to Princess Margaret, who is a distant cousin to Princess Tatiana.

Oh yes, I almost forgot, the only condition attached to the bequest was that the aviary should contain, at the very least, one Indian myna bird, who would be responsible for running the joint.

LAWRENCE OF ARABIA
AND THE
BEDOUIN'S CAT SHOES

Of Sophia Shebaldin what is there to say? The top letter writer of them all seemed to have been written out. All the letters she wrote for Cleopatra's Cat to her children must have cured her of letter writing forever. Perhaps, with all that had happened to her, just the mere act of writing a letter brought back too many painful memories. The news Mrs Moses received of her was secondhand and not very much at that. It came from the professor, who wasn't very good at gossip or remembering the things women wanted to know. He had accompanied Sophia Shebaldin to England and had also managed to find her a ginger kitten, the pick of a litter belonging to a ginger tabby, a longtime resident of Magdalen College, Oxford. True to her word, Sophia christened it Sir Frederick Treves, purchased a cat basket at Liberty's, and bought a second-class cabin ticket on a steamer bound for Port Said.

The first news of her continued existence came five years after the First World War when Colonel Lawrence of Arabia was interviewed by the BBC radio program, 'Traveller's Tales'. The interviewer, perhaps hoping to get the program under way in a controversial way, remarked on the fact that Lawrence was wearing a most curious-looking pair of open sandals in the middle of an English winter.

Lawrence laughed. 'Oh, you mean my cat shoes.'

'Do you have a problem with your feet, Colonel Lawrence?' the BBC man inquired. 'Perhaps a legacy from fighting in the desert with the Bedouin tribesmen?'

'Good heavens, no! In fact, entirely the opposite is the case,' Lawrence exclaimed. Then he told the story of how he had been presented with the sandals by an elder among the Bedouins. 'The sandals he gave me were quite different from the ubiquitous

Egyptian toe sandal,' Lawrence explained, adding that his Bedouin host had called the sandals 'cat shoes', and it was obvious that they were held in high regard by the old Arab.

The sandals, while being somewhat different in their strapping arrangement, more European in design than Arab, were most curiously different in the construction of the sole. For instance, the upper side of the leather sole was contorted or shaped with the arch built up on the inside of the instep so that the effect was to completely support the arch, the sandal seemed to naturally mould to the contour of the foot. Furthermore the upper side of the sole, that is to say the surface upon which the foot rested, was covered with hundreds of little leather nodules. This meant that when you slipped them on, it was somewhat disconcerting as the nodules pressed into the sole of the foot for a decidedly uncomfortable result.

The old man had grinned knowingly when Lawrence, having slipped the sandals on, made a wry face as he attempted to walk.

Lawrence knew he could not possibly reject the sandals, they were a gift not given lightly, nor could he refrain from wearing them for fear of insulting his host. So he was forced to make the best of a bad situation and to persevere with the strange footwear through one long, very hot day.

That evening in the privacy of his tent he removed what he had come to think of in the course of the day as his torture sandals, an example of yet another of the many crosses he was obliged to bear in the name of good Anglo–Arab relations.

However, as he sat on his bedding to remove the footwear he realised that, curiously, since mid-afternoon he'd quite forgotten about their existence. Now when he'd removed the Bedouin's cat shoes he realised that his feet seemed much less tired than usual. The camel he had been riding that day had developed a limp and he had been obliged to walk a great distance across the hot sand, and now, surprisingly, his feet felt better than he could ever remember.

When the opportunity arose, Lawrence of Arabia asked his Bedouin host about the sandals, thinking them to be some ancient secret of Bedouin leather craft. Instead he was told that the sandals were made by a Russian woman who lived alone with a red cat in the small town of El Burumbul, some two hundred and fifty kilometres from Cairo. The

Bedouin elder then went on to tell Lawrence of Arabia the curious tale of the origin of the cat shoes.

One day, several years previously, a young Bedouin goat herd had badly sprained his ankle while chasing a goat and was in such terrible pain that he was quite unable to walk. After dragging himself along for some distance he was finally overcome by the heat and lay helpless in the blistering midday sun. He wasn't anywhere near the Bedouin camp and was also without water, having removed the goatskin gourd strung across his shoulders so as to make it easier to chase the goat. Now as he lay in a delirium, where he would certainly have perished in a few more hours, a strange woman, a white woman wearing a large straw hat, suddenly emerged, seemingly out of nowhere. She lifted the young boy onto her back and carried him more than a kilometre to a small mud hovel, taking the urchin into the dark, cool interior of her home. She bathed his forehead until he became conscious, then she commenced to work on his sprain. So effective was her treatment that by evening, with the help of a stick, he was able to return to the camp, to the great joy of everyone, around midnight.

The goats had returned at sunset of their own accord and the boy's family and other members of the tribe had immediately set out to look for him. They were hampered by a new moon but eventually they came upon his water bag and judging from its contents they decided the lad had not taken water since about ten that morning. From this fact they concluded that if he was not dead by now he would be wandering in the desert quite delirious. They had reluctantly returned home, having given him up for lost. In fact, the Bedouin women had already begun their keening, knowing that if he was not already dead, the night, when the temperature often gets down below freezing, would finish him off.

Without water or the means to make a fire, the young goat boy would most certainly perish. In the morning they would watch the sky for circling vultures so that they might find his body to bury it. 'There had been,' the old Arab said, 'great rejoicing when the boy entered the camp with the stars at the zenith.'

The following day his father had gone to the woman's tiny house to thank her for his son's safe return and, as a token of his gratitude, he had presented her with a small sack of dates and dried apricots. The woman, who had not covered her face at his approach and who seemed not to understand why he had come, at first refused the gift. But when he had insisted, even showing some anger at her refusal, she had changed her mind. Then, much to the man's embarrassment, she had neutralised his gift with a pair of curious-looking sandals, pressing them into his reluctant hands and then pointing to his feet.

Like Lawrence, the man could not refuse her gift without insulting the white lady who, though an infidel, had saved his son's life. So, he had returned with them to the camp where he told of the red cat and the woman infidel, who wore a great hat of plaited grass and dared to show her face to a male stranger.

Everyone shook their heads in dismay at the woman's boldness of manner, but then had enjoyed a good laugh at the notion of the ridiculous-looking sandals. More in jest than anything else, and because he had supplied them all with a great deal of entertainment, the boy's father, thinking to stretch the attention he had received a bit further, had worn the strange sandals for a few hours. Like Lawrence, he discovered that the sandals possessed some sort of magic healing power.

To cut a long story short, all the Bedouins started wearing them. Soon the strange lady with her red cat had a small but thriving business going among the tribesmen.

The Bedouin elder spread his hands and gave Lawrence an almost toothless smile, 'That is the story of your sandals, Lourens effendi. We still get the cat shoes from this white woman with the red cat.'

Lawrence was aware of the ability of the Bedouins to fashion almost anything with their hands. 'But why do you not make them for yourselves?' he asked.

The elder looked shocked. 'You do not understand, Lourens, it is the red cat, the magic red cat. Have you seen how a cat walks, silent, perfectly balanced, as though on air? A cat's paws are always cool, it is the same with the cat shoes the woman makes, there is magic in them, a magic we cannot copy for fear of Allah's wrath that we should steal an idea from an infidel.'

Lawrence of Arabia then told the man from the BBC how he took the sandals back to England, where he wore them increasingly until the idea of wearing a sensible pair of English brogues became anathema to him. He had come slowly to realise that what happened to your feet largely decides the degree of your general wellbeing. He told the man on the radio that his cat shoes proved to be almost indestructible and when the soles wore thin he simply resoled them. Now the cat shoes were simply the footwear he preferred and, as often as not, he wore them with a collar and tie and his Sunday best suit. The local people in the village in which he lived eventually came to accept the sandals as a sign of his growing eccentricity. That is until a chance conversation occurred between himself and a visiting Swiss chiropodist.

It seemed a certain Dr Scholl had come to visit a neighbour and had been introduced to Lawrence. The foot doctor had noted Lawrence's sandals and, like the BBC man, had questioned why he preferred to wear them. Lawrence had removed a sandal, or cat shoe as he called it, and handed it to the famous chiropodist, at the same time vouching for its efficacy.

The Swiss foot doctor had asked if he might see both cat shoes and then examined them with great interest, rubbing his thumb up and down the hundreds of tiny leather nodules that covered the surface of the inner sole.

'It is so obvious!' he exclaimed in a surprised voice. 'So very obvious!' He clapped his palm against his forehead, 'Why did I not think myself of this?' He looked up at Lawrence, 'My dear Colonel Lawrence, are you aware that every nerve in the human body ends in the feet?' He ran his thumb over the myriad little nodules again, 'These sharp little bumps seem to act as a constant massage, stimulating the blood flow through the feet and up into the body.'

He returned the sandals to Colonel Lawrence and, removing his glasses, began to polish them nervously with a clean white handkerchief that he produced from the inside pocket of his jacket. 'Wunderbar! Wonderful!' His eyes positively shone. 'Ja, we shall see what I can do with this idea! You are a genius, Colonel Lawrence!'

'Not me, my dear fellow, some Russian woman in the Arabian desert who lives with a ginger cat, she's your genius.'

Sophia Shebaldin was never heard of again, but around the mid-1930s the Bedouin were observed to no longer wear cat shoes. One can only surmise that she must have passed away and that the tribesmen were too superstitious to copy her magic sandals.

As for Dr Scholl, the chiropodist who had visited Lawrence? His is by now a well-known success story.

Of Sir Frederick Treves, the ginger cat, nothing is also known. Except that if you should visit the pyramids in El Giza, you will notice the presence of a great many cats which, since time out of mind, have been regarded by Egyptians to be sacred animals. It is surprising how many of these creatures are distinctly ginger in colour.

THE MECHANIC

AND THE

MAID FROM THE ASTRA HOTEL

I have left the story of what happened to Mr Petrov of the beluga caviar fame until last, not because it is the most dramatic story of them all, but because it is the one that affects me the most.

As was always expected, Mr Petrov made a bee-line for New York where he would meet his five sisters and his beloved Katya Markova of the scorpion sting.

But perhaps the scorpion had left some of its nature behind in the poison it had injected into the slim and pretty ankle of Mr Petrov's proposed bride. Because when he eventually arrived, he was met by his five sisters, who had waited for seven hours outside the immigration processing shed on New York's Ellis Island to welcome their brother to America, but of Katya Markova there was no sign.

Mr Petrov, always polite, held each of his loving sisters in his arms and amid copious tears they welcomed him to the land of the free. It was only after a long ride to the Lower East Side in a modern internal-combustion motor called an omnibus that he asked about Katya Markova.

For some moments his sisters were silent, each reluctant to be the one to tell him but then the eldest, Nadia, spoke. 'She met a banker named J.P. Morgan, Jnr,' she said tentatively.

'So who is this Morgan?' Mr Petrov asked. 'What has he done to Katya?'

'She is his mistress!' they all cried and then collectively burst into tears.

'Mistress? What is a mistress?'

'His fancy woman,' Nadia said quietly.

Mr Petrov could hardly believe his ears. 'But she is promised to me, we are betrothed.'

'This is America, my brother, the old rules do not apply here,' Nadia answered, averting her eyes from those of her brother.

'He is an old man of fifty years, he gave her a fur

coat and a diamond ring!' Natasha, the youngest, exclaimed. 'She has also an automobile and a chauffeur and a nice brownstone house!'

'I will kill him!' Mr Petrov swore.

But Mr Petrov did no such thing. Instead he got a job on the waterfront in the fish markets and found, increasingly, that while life in America was good, he kept thinking about Mrs Moses, who was no beauty like Katya Markova but with whom he seemed to have formed such a good partnership on the road.

He also discovered that each of his sisters had a beau, as the Americans called it, a young man who sought their hand in marriage. They had all refrained from accepting the various proposals, waiting for their brother to arrive to give his permission and blessing to the match. Nadia, for instance, had waited nearly three years, much to the chagrin of the widower shopkeeper who was to be her intended.

Mr Petrov could find no fault in any of the suitors and agreed that each of his sisters had his permission to wed. After all, he told himself, in Russia, with the furore over his so-called affair with Katya Markova and the spoiled caviar, they would have remained spinsters for the rest of their lives. Here in America they could start a new life and have families of their own.

Nadia, despite being the first to find a sweetheart, was the last to wed, attending first to the wedding arrangements of all of her sisters and seeing that they brought a small dowry with them. Each had a traditional wedding in the Russian Orthodox Church in Stuyvesant and, although these were modest enough affairs, Mr Petrov had to work for three years to pay for the wedding feasts. Finally Nadia took the vows, though not before she told Mr Petrov that she was prepared to give up her fiancé if he required her to look after him.

With all five of his sisters married and after five years in America Mr Petrov was drafted into the United States Army where they trained him as a motor mechanic and sent him to fight in France and Germany, where he was twice mentioned in despatches.

Back in New York after the war Mr Petrov bought a small fish shop with a war veteran's grant, but found he couldn't settle down. Finally, he admitted to himself that he must act on something that had been scratching away at his heart ever since he'd come away from Russia. He sold the fish shop to an Italian migrant and had sufficient money for the boat trip to Australia and a handsome gold and diamond engagement ring.

Three months later, with the waves lapping on the white sand, and just on sunset, he proposed to Mrs Moses while they were walking along Bondi Beach. Mrs Moses immediately accepted, she had always loved Mr Petrov but had never dared to think that he may have reciprocated her feelings.

'Papa went on his knees,' she'd exclaimed to me, 'in the wet sand and he asked to marry me. I thought, "Oh my God! Maybe I die and gone to heaven already."'

Because Mr Petrov wasn't a Jew they were married at the registry office in the city, where Whacker O'Sullivan was called upon to be the best man and chief witness. Almost all the Irish and, in fact, most of the permanent population of Bondi Beach came to the wedding, invited or not. A Russian-Irish-Australian wedding is no affair for the timid and a grand and somewhat drunken time was had by all. Well after midnight three local crims and the mayor of Waverley carried Sergeant Bumper O'Flynn home in a deck chair they'd collapsed to use as a stretcher.

For a while Mrs Moses attempted to call herself Mrs Petrov, but as Mr Petrov called her Mrs Moses as did everyone else, she finally gave up and resumed her old identity.

Immediately after the Great War there were plenty of jobs for blacksmiths in Australia, but from his very first ride in an omnibus in New York, Mr Petrov had fallen in love with the internal-combustion engine. His war experience had turned him into a first-rate mechanic and so, with Mrs Moses's savings made as a cook at the Astra Hotel, Mr Petrov and Mrs Moses bought a tin shed at the corner of Curlewis Street and Campbell Parade and turned it into a combination garage and smithy.

For several years they lived in two fibro rooms behind the garage until they had sufficient to buy a home on the point overlooking the beach. They were blessed with a daughter, who, because of a Jewish mother, retained her faith, maintaining it into her marriage. Her daughter too had a daughter, who eventually became my wife.

I am the cook in our family and every Friday morning, just after dawn, I drive to the fish markets and buy a big snapper. By nine a.m. it is scaled, filleted and cooked, the head and the tail put aside for soup. People who try my fish often comment that it is quite the best they've tasted. I always thank them politely and then add, 'I'm afraid it has nothing whatsoever to do with me, my fish is cooked in a frying pan possessed of a Russian soul.'

OTHER BOOKS BY
BRYCE COURTENAY

THE POWER OF ONE

Born in a South Africa divided by racism and hatred, young Peekay will come to lead all the tribes of Africa. Through enduring friendships, he gains the strength he needs to win out. And in a final conflict with his childhood enemy, Peekay will fight to the death for justice . . .

Bryce Courtenay's classic bestseller is a story of triumph of the human spirit – a spellbinding tale for all ages.

TANDIA

Tandia is a child of all Africa: half Indian, half African, beautiful and intelligent, she is only sixteen when she is first brutalised by the police. Her fear of the white man leads her to join the black resistance movement, where she trains as a terrorist.

With her in the fight for justice is the one white man Tandia can trust, the welterweight champion of the world, Peekay. Now he must fight their common enemy in order to save both their lives.

THE AUSTRALIAN TRILOGY
THE POTATO FACTORY

Ikey Solomon and his partner in crime, Mary Abacus, make the harsh journey from thriving nineteenth-century London to the convict settlement of Van Diemen's Land. In the back-streets and dives of Hobart Town, Mary builds The Potato Factory, where she plans a new future. But her ambitions are threatened by Ikey's wife, Hannah, her old enemy. As each woman sets out to destroy the other, the families are brought to the edge of disaster.

TOMMO & HAWK

Brutally kidnapped and separated in childhood, Tommo and Hawk are reunited in Hobart Town. Together they escape their troubled pasts and set off on a journey into manhood. From whale hunting in the Pacific to the Maori wars in New Zealand, from the Rocks in Sydney to the miners' riots at the goldfields, Tommo and Hawk must learn each other's strengths and weaknesses in order to survive.

SOLOMON'S SONG

When Mary Abacus dies, she leaves her business empire in the hands of the warring Solomon family. Hawk Solomon is determined to bring together both sides of the tribe – but it is the new generation who must fight to change the future. Solomons are pitted against Solomons as the families are locked in a bitter struggle that crosses battlefields and continents to reach a powerful conclusion.

JESSICA

Jessica is based on the inspiring true story of a young girl's fight for justice against tremendous odds. A tomboy, Jessica is the pride of her father, as they work together on the struggling family farm. One quiet day, the peace of the bush is devastated by a terrible murder. Only Jessica is able to save the killer from the lynch mob – but will justice prevail in the courts?

Nine months later, a baby is born . . . with Jessica determined to guard the secret of the father's identity. The rivalry of Jessica and her beautiful sister for the love of the same man will echo throughout their lives – until finally the truth must be told.

Set in a harsh Australian bush against the outbreak of World War I, this novel is heartbreaking in its innocence, and shattering in its brutality.

SMOKY JOE'S CAFE

Thommo returns from Vietnam to an Australia that regards him as a mercenary guilty of war crimes. All who remain of his platoon who fought and died in the Battle of Long Tan are affected the same way. Now Thommo and his mates are angry men out for revenge. They're the 'Dirty Dozen', just like the movie. Only it's real life, and they're so screwed up they probably couldn't fight their way out of a wet paper bag.

That is, until a woman of character steps in. Wendy's infant daughter is dying and needs a bone-marrow transplant. Hell hath no fury . . . as she sets out to mould this bunch of ex-jungle fighters into a unit that will fight for justice, by fair means or foul.

APRIL FOOL'S DAY

Damon Courtenay died on the morning of April Fool's Day. In this tribute to his son, Bryce Courtenay lays bare the suffering behind this young man's life. Damon's story is one of lifelong struggle, his love for Celeste, the compassion of family, and a fight to the end for integrity.

A testimony to the power of love, *April Fool's Day* is also about understanding: how when we confront our worst, we can become our best.

This life-affirming book will change the way you think.